I0547871

FROM THE BOOK

"Those who truly love justice will always stand with me against the evil of tyrants who wrap all of you in bondage to greed and judgemental arrogance. I have suffered mightily because in the face of deceit, truth becomes revolutionary." (*The Son of Thunder*)

"This man was talking sedition. He was suggesting that people should question authority." (*F.B.I. Agent*)

No one knew from where he came. One day in April of 2006, he simply appeared, strolling down the cracked sidewalks of Main Street, the boarded up buildings seemingly a worthy compliment to his unkempt nature. He was moderately tall, comely, with a very irreverent countenance, such that those who saw him would respect him, but there was also an element of this man to fear, made plain by his assured manner of gliding wilfully down the nearly deserted street. (*Description of the Son of Thunder*)

Her rash hand held the weapon of deceit. Forth from the vine she spread the evil fruit. Earth felt the wound she inflicted. Rising from darkness, she spit fire. (*Sidewalk Annie*)

As the Son of Thunder

The Author

Wayne Frye's Aaron Adams series has been popular among Canadian mystery lovers since first appearing in 2005. He provides satirical political commentary to many Canadian newspapers, and his books on politics have created a great deal of controversy. He has written marketing/ advertising textbooks, been a successful U.S. university hockey coach, and served as a marketing consultant to hockey teams and motion picture companies. He has been cited for his work with inner-city gang children in the Los Angeles area, and is a fervent supporter of the anti-globalization movement. He became a Canadian citizen in 2003 and lives with his wife in Ladysmith, British Columbia.

Other Books by J. Wayne Frye

Guide to Local Radio and Television Copywriting
Something Evil in the Darkness at Hopkins House
How Hockey Saved a Jew From the Holocaust:
The Rudi Ball Story
The Catastrophic Calamities of a Village Idiot
Fighting for Justice in the Land of Hypocrisy
Guide to Alternative Education (13 Editions)
Cataclysmic Dreams in Black and White
Mastering Marketing Research
Introduction to Advertising
Marketing Plan Work Book
Public Relations Workbook
The Fall From Apocalypse
Advertising Lab Manual
Promotions Workbook
Advertising Design
Armageddon Now
Worth

Books Written With Jasmine H. Frye

Canadian Angels of Mercy: Nurses in Times of Peril

As the Son of Thunder

WHEN JESUS CAME
TO JERSEY
AS THE SON OF THUNDER

By
J. Wayne Frye

To Monte

Because of his love and concern for me, he sent me a video to guide me toward the light, as he perceives it. Although the effect was the opposite of what he intended, it did serve as a catalyst for this book. We must all seek the light – the light that makes us rage against the evil of greed and intolerance that binds us in invisible chains to our government, corporate and religious masters.

TABLE OF CONTENTS

When Jesus Came to Jersey

Catalogue Number: 20126196108

ISBN: 978-0-9735973-8-7

Peninsula Publishing

Fireside Books – Victoria, BC - Canada

As the Son of Thunder

PROLOGUE
THE SON OF THUNDER
IN THE LAND OF HYPOCRISY

The Bible says that the truth will set you free. Well, Aaron Adams had learned the truth, and it was not the truth most people wanted to hear. In his hands was the new *New Testament*. Aaron was in possession of a document more important than the *Dead Sea Scrolls*. This was going to shake the foundations of Christianity, because this was an account of Jesus by Jesus, an account that the church and the American government wanted to suppress, because the truth was too explosive for the power structure to accept. If the truth got out, those who manipulated and controlled the religious masses would see their power diminished. Muslim, Christian and Jew would all look at the religious hierarchy with disdain, because what had been taught was actually an abomination, rather than a guiding light for salvation.

Aaron looked out the window that read, *A. Adams – Private Investigator*, as blood flowed from the wound in his side like water over Niagara Falls. He faced a dire dilemma that could irrevocably change a society that he had held in extreme contempt ever since he was old enough

As the Son of Thunder

to realize that the rich and powerful in America and most other countries used religion to control the masses and lead them down the path of exploitation.

Coming up in the south during the civil rights era, Aaron had seen how religion was used to stir up the white masses against integration. The pastors in the white churches had used the Bible's story of the tribe of Ham as justification for the separation of the races. God, himself, had sanctioned the separation of the races according to these pontificating purveyors of deceit. How many times had Aaron heard the refrain, "you have to protect yourself from the niggers and non-believers, because they will lead you down the path of eternal damnation." He remembered the sign he once read as he crossed into Alabama on a family trip, "Welcome to Alabama: Niggers, Jews and Catholics keep out."

One would think a society that elected African Americans to political offices had overcome the evils of racism. Well, some people had overcome it, but they had never overcome the manipulation that kept most Americans mired in subjugation to patriotic babble and religious subterfuge. Those at the seats of power had used racism as a means to consolidate their control, and these same people

8

As the Son of Thunder

had also used religion as a manipulative tool to keep the masses in line.

The Bible said, "the meek shall inherit the earth." Unfortunately, the people quoting that phrase already controlled the earth and saw to it that their progeny would continue that control after they were gone. It was not the meek who would inherit the earth, but the offspring of the rich and powerful who continued the nepotism from one generation to another. Meanwhile, the poor slobs who listened to manipulative scripture from pontificating ministers of deceit fell submissively in line and walked to the slaughter.

What Aaron held in his hand could change all that. He had the real Biblical truths right there in a text directly from the source, Jesus himself, rather than the texts that had been filtered through the eyes of the church for so long. Aaron could blow the lid off the corrupt, manipulative, truth-hiding government and church. Jesus may have been portrayed as meek in the New Testament, but in Aaron's document, he was not just God's son, he was a revolutionary, wild-eyed anarchist bent on bringing down the hypocrisy that permeated the very soul of humanity. Jesus was more than the son of God, he was the son of thunder in the land of hypocrisy.

9

CHAPTER 1
THE BEGINNING

It was a warm, humid night in Little Rock, Arkansas when Aaron Adams was picked up at the airport by fellow private eye, Dixon Long. He had flown down from New York at the behest of his old army buddy. Dixon had insisted Aaron tell no one where he was going or whom he was meeting.

As they made their way through the backcountry, seemingly leaving civilization behind, they pulled up to an isolated, dilapidated cabin. Making their way to the front door, then going inside, they continued their discussion from the car of how America, under the leadership of that monumental buffoon, George Bush, had literally been made into a third world country to benefit the corporations. Commenting on the continuous wars of conquest, they begin to feel that old kinship spawned by their mutual hatred of an economic system based on greed. That old spark of mutual admiration was kindled by two men who stood for social justice in a country that only believed in the exploitation of workers for the benefit of corporations.

Along with that exploitation was a commitment to proselytizing about the compatibility of pure

10

Christianity and capitalism. Meanwhile, the church sat idly by as Americans were denied health care. The same churches did nothing to protest the war crimes committed for many years by George Bush and his henchmen who decided torture conducted by America was not torture but merely legitimate use of force. Other countries tortured but not America. Churches never exhorted disagreement with a tax system that gave the rich a free ride on the backs of the middle class and poor. Christians sat back without a whimper about a nation that had the largest gap between the rich and poor in the entire industrialized world. And while America incarcerated more people than any other country, they were ranting against abortion and homosexuality rather than cruel and unusual punishment. Aaron, the ethereal atheist, was about to learn something from Dixon Long that would make the Christian hierarchy fear for their very existence.

As they lifted their glasses in a toast, Aaron could not help but notice that Dixon had aged greatly since they last were together more than ten years ago, but it was not that he had just aged. There was a deep seated anger in his eyes, almost as if he was ready to explode with an emotional tirade of fury. Dixon was in pain, and that was why Aaron was there.

11

"Aaron, I am going to tell you a story that you will not believe. I know you are an atheist, and I respect your beliefs, but I must insist that you respect mine, and although I am not asking you to put aside your disdain for religion, I am asking you to at least consider the possibility that there might have been a Jesus at one time."

Aaron was not one to willingly suffer the arrogance and self-righteousness of Christians. Yet, he was respectful of people like Dixon, who were religious, but never looked at themselves as the sole possessors of righteousness. For that reason, he respectfully replied, "Dixon, I think you all believe in nothing more than fairy tales, but I am certainly respectful of your beliefs, and you have never let your beliefs interfere with your compassion for those who suffer at the altar of self-righteous Christians. You are a Christian who refuses to let that little black book filled with evil do your thinking for you. If all Christians were like you, this could be a country that moves forward rather than being stuck in the Middle Ages, where people still want to have the morals police out accosting individuals for any violation of the proscribed code of behaviour as defined by the pompous purveyors of deceit who proclaim themselves the interpreters of God's word. In a country where people see images of Jesus in a

12

grilled cheese sandwich and bow down to worship it, you are a voice for reason. I respect you. Although I cannot put aside my belief that Christianity is nothing more than an invention of the rich and powerful to manipulate and control the masses who are not smart enough to think for themselves, I will do all in my power to put in abeyance my disdain for religion, if it will let me help you."

"Aaron, I have met Jesus. I know you won't believe me, but I have seen him, my friend. I spent time with him."

Aaron, ever the skeptic, grinned slightly and said, "So you want me to believe that you have seen Jesus? People see him in grilled cheese sandwiches, toilet bowls, jelly, potatoes and tortillas. One woman even claimed his face appeared on her ass. Now that is the one I want to see. Get real Dixon. All these people are too steeped in fantasies to realize that there was never a painting of Jesus. All the visions look like the way he is imagined by artists. People's lives are so mundane and miserable that they long for some type of pie in the sky. Most hope that there is something much better for them after they suffer through this life. Dixon, I know you are smarter than that."

13

Dixon leaned forward and picked up a tattered piece of paper from the coffee table. Handing it to Aaron, he said, "This was given to me by a man who died in my arms, defending the sanctity of Jesus, who has been spirited away by a government that fears him more than the Pharisees ever did.

Aaron stared at the tattered paper that was a small portion of what had been a pack of Winston cigarettes. Looking at the Winston logo on the front, he did not even think about turning it over until Dixon said, "Look on the back."

On the plain inside back in red ink was one sentence. *Matthew, remember that I am the light and salvation for all mankind. Jesus, son of Mary.*

Fighting back laughter out of respect for his dear friend, Aaron quizzically struggled for words and all that would come out was, "this is bullshit Dixon. Come on."

Dixon leaned over, reached under the chair, pulled out a spiral notebook and handed it to Aaron. He got up, stared down at him and said, "I am going to bed. Read that and we will talk in the morning. What you have in your hands is not the end. It is just the beginning."

14

As the Son of Thunder

CHAPTER 2
I AM THE LIGHT

Opening the spiral binder, Aaron squinted his eyes at a very difficult to read handwritten series of notes, but the first few lines were clearly discernable, as it was written in bold letters that had been traced over several times to make them stand out. Then, they had been underlined to reinforce their significance.

I, Jesus of Nazareth hereby proclaim that what follows is to be the new, New Testament. All that has gone before is to be discarded, as it is an abomination of my words funnelled through the eyes of those who would use me as a means to manipulate and control the populace in order to serve narrow self-interests and to keep the masses in bondage to a vile and inhuman system of economic and spiritual bondage. I have come back to offer true salvation to all who will heed my words and rise up in rebellion against the imprisonment of the world to those who would trample on the innate rights of all humanity in order to enslave the many for the benefit of the few.

Do not mistake the truth that follows. It is time that humanity knew the real Jesus.

15

Those who turn to me must realize that I offer hope, but that hope can only be realized by individuals who are willing to stand against the tyranny of the barons of greed who rule the world and the false profits of power who fill the churches of America with abominations of my Father's words. Remember that when I was on earth 2000 years ago, I told all who would listen that what had gone before was to be discarded. The Old Testament was written, not by my Father, but by those who wanted to control the masses of the day by binding them to the superstitious power of a vengeful God. My Father is not vengeful. That is why he allows those who proclaim themselves His servants to denigrate all for which he stands as they continue with their blasphemous assault on the true meaning of His words. He refuses to smite those who have enslaved the masses to the evil of capitalist exploitation. He has sent me again, this time to America for the second time, as I have been sent many times before to all parts of the world to rally the marginalized of this planet to rise up against greed and subjugation by the powerful and wealthy. Rarely have I succeeded in moving the marginalized of the world to throw off their shackles and stand in the glory of freedom from want and fear. Most times, these people are not willing to end their own slavery, so why should my beloved Father in heaven give them what they

16

are unwilling to fight for themselves. He is a loving God, but he is a God who demands people take responsibility for their own plight. Allowing the greedy and powerful to rule is a choice individuals make on their own by refusing to fight for justice. God has given everyone the power to change things, but complacency is the reason he has sent me again to try and rally the hungry, the marginalized and the forgotten ones to stand together and tear down the wall of greed in this nation that allows the few to accumulate vast riches on the backs of the many. This is an abomination in the eyes of my Father in heaven, but it is not He who will end it. It is each one of you to whom he has given the power to destroy this evil. I will show you the way as directed by Him, but I will not do for you that which He has given you the power to do for yourself. Anarchy is evil according to those in power, but anarchy put in the hands of those who would lead you out of despair is not anarchy at all – it is freedom. I will give you the keys to open the door of true economic and social freedom, but you must be willing to fight with all your strength against the guardians of the status-quo who dare stand in the way of your God-given right to live an abundant life free of want, turmoil and disorder. I am truly the light that will brighten the darkness of despair promulgated by those who love darkness.

17

Aaron placed the binder on the coffee table and fought back laughter. Yet, he had to give it to this guy, whoever he was, for being a different pretender to the throne of God. At least he was not preaching supplication and bowing to authority. This was a Jesus Aaron could dig, even if he was a fake. This was a man who knew that nothing is accomplished by complacency and non-violence in a nation that used violence to force its will on all who stood in its way, whether within the country or without. The jails were filled with those who dared question authority. Yet, here was a man claiming that God sanctioned anarchy when standing against the authority of the power structure.

Aaron had read enough for now. Leaving the notebook open at the last page, he tossed it onto the coffee table. He had to get some sleep. Eschewing the bedroom, he eased off his shoes and pivoted to lie down on the sofa. He looked to his right at the spiral notebook, still open to the last page he read. It seemed to flutter in a non-existent breeze. His eyes moved toward the bottom of the last page he had read, and in small script in the margin the words scribbled there seemed to leap off the page. *I am the light. I am the light.*

18

CHAPTER 3
THE GAME IS AFOOT

Aaron was awakened as two men barged through the front door. No knock, just two burly guys who tore the door from its hinges. The biggest one moved toward the sofa, gun in hand, spitting lead as Aaron rolled onto the floor. Hitting the coffee table and somehow getting slightly under it was a lucky break, because it altered the trajectory of the bullet that only grazed his left shoulder. Having no gun of his own, the aging Aaron summoned the strength of a younger man to mightily kick the coffee table into the guy's path. As the hulking, burly menace tried to push the coffee table aside, Aaron's survival instincts kicked into overdrive. Rising from the floor like Poseidon from the depths of the deepest ocean, he grabbed the wine bottle that had fallen to the floor, lowered his head and dived forward, hitting the guy square in the chest, causing the gun to fall to the floor, while Aaron bashed the guy's head in like a ripe watermelon with the bottle. As he made gurgling death sounds, Aaron's right hand somehow found its way around the nearby gun that had fallen to the floor.

Meanwhile, the other guy encountered Dixon as he came out of the bedroom to see what was going

19

on. Dixon was stopped in his tracks by a bullet that ripped into his abdomen, sending him sprawling against the door frame. In a partially sitting position, staring quizzically at his assailant, he knew that it was all over for him. Just as he was about to utter the words, "fuck you," the top of the man's head exploded as a bullet fired by Aaron splattered brains and bone fragments all over the wall.

Aaron rushed to Dixon's side. Looking down at him, he knew that there was no hope. The gapping wound had ripped all the way through Dixon's mid-section, leaving his intestines spilling out onto the floor. Dixon just looked up at Aaron with a partial smile creeping across his lips and said, "these fuckers are just the first. They want that binder. Don't let them get it. Protect it, and protect the man who wrote it. Woodbury - Woodbury, New Jersey."

Dixon died in Aaron's arms. His old friend seemed at peace. Adjusting Dixon's body from a sitting position, Aaron lay him on the floor, walked into the bedroom and pulled a sheet off the bed. Going back into the living room, he gently placed the sheet over his friend, and grimaced as the blood from the mortal wound seeped through the white sheet.

20

As the Son of Thunder

The two thugs who had barged into the home were not worthy of respect in death, so Aaron made no attempt to cover their bodies. He bent over the one who had killed Dixon, rolled him over on his stomach and reached into the killer's back pocket and removed his wallet. Flipping it open, there encased in a plastic window was an ID. And what an ID. The official-looking gold embossed ID read, *Curtis Cruston, Special Agent, FBI.*

Walking over to the other body and removing his wallet, Aaron's jaw dropped as he read, *Niles Trupp, Special Agent, FBI.* Aaron had killed, not just one FBI agent, but two. Trouble had come calling.

No one knew Aaron was in Arkansas, but there was a record of his airline ticket. It would not take long for the Feds to uncover his friendship with Dixon. He could get out of town and hope for the best, or he could stay put, call the authorities and tell them what happened. Sure, tell the authorities you killed two FBI agents who barged in unannounced, shot your friend and would have undoubtedly killed you given the chance. Further reflection made Aaron realize that the gulags of America were filled with people who believed the authorities were fair and just. He was going to

21

wipe the place clean of his prints and haul ass out of there.

Walking onto the porch, Aaron wondered where the FBI agents had parked their car. Only Dixon's old Ford Escort was in the driveway. The quiet seemed almost deafening. Scanning the area, ever vigilant of what might be awaiting in the darkness, he crouched a bit and held the gun he had taken from the FBI agent close to his side, cocked and ready.

The car's engine roared to life, reverberating loudly in the intense quiet of the surrounding forest. Just as he started to put it in reverse, he remembered the binder and how Dixon had pleaded with his dying breath for Aaron to protect it. Returning to the cabin, he removed the binder and got back in the car. As he proceeded down the dirt road, he passed a black sedan parked to the side about 200 feet from the cabin. No doubt, they had parked the car there to avoid detection, but what did the FBI want with Dixon, or could they have been after Aaron? They could not have been after Aaron, no one knew he was there but Dixon.

After five minutes that seemed like hours, Aaron turned left onto the highway. The highway was empty, but as he looked at the horizon over an approaching hill, he could see a string of headlights headed his way. At the top of the hill, the black sedans, three of them with four men in dark suits in each one, streaked by at a high speed. Constantly glaring in his rear view mirror, breathing heavily with anxiety, he feared that the cars might turn around and follow him. They were government cars. There was no doubt about that, and he had just killed two FBI agents.

Aaron had killed before. Many times in Vietnam, it had been sanctioned by a government that told the 19 year old Aaron that he was defending America from those Godless commies. Yeah, like all brainwashed patriots, Aaron had swallowed the propaganda until he saw what was really going on. He and Dixon found out the hard way that those who blindly serve are nothing but chumps being led to the slaughter by moneyed interests who profit from the patriotic servitude imposed on the poor. Well, Aaron had killed again, and it was justified. Yet, try telling that to the Feds. Ask people like Leonard Peltier, who was railroaded by the government in a vendetta to avenge the deaths of two FBI agents at Wounded Knee, if the government is ever on the side of those who dare question its authority. The jails of America were filled with those who dared stand-up for justice and fairness.

23

Aaron's return ticket was for the next morning at 10:00 AM. Should he wait? Should he try to get out of Little Rock now? One thing he had to do was dump the car. No doubt those three cars he passed on the highway were headed toward Dixon's and filled with more FBI men. By now the airport, bus stations, train stations and all roads out of town would be covered. He had to think. Seeing a McDonald's, he pulled in, parked the car and stealthily meandered down the street toward a flashing neon sign that read, Marion Hotel. Checking in as Matt Sotae, Aaron paid in cash, so there would be no credit card record. Obviously, from the looks of the place, this was not the kind of motel that really cared about checking ID's.

Turning on the television, Aaron reclined on the bed and kept switching through channels, searching for any news about the killing of two FBI agents. He finally drifted off to sleep thinking about Dixon, whose last words were Woodbury, New Jersey.

Awaking the next morning at exactly 7:00 AM, the TV was still on and the local morning news headline, delivered by the usual attractive, silken haired newswoman, who probably got her training in modeling school, was "local private detective perishes in house fire."

24

There was no mention of any FBI agents being killed, and nothing about Dixon being shot. Just a short report that said the fire department had responded to a call indicating a cabin was burning off Ozark Road. Found in the cabin were the charred remains of Little Rock private detective, Dixon Long. Preliminary investigation indicated that he had fallen asleep with a cigarette in his hands. Typical government bumbling. They were too stupid to check to see that Dixon Long did not smoke.

So, the FBI was covering up the deaths of two agents. Why? What would be the government's motive for not revealing what would be termed the murder of two agents?

Aaron quickly showered and decided it would be safe to take a plane out of Little Rock. The FBI was covering something up, and not revealing the killing of two of its agents meant it was big, really big. And in the middle of it all was Aaron Adams. Aaron thought that as Sherlock Holmes used to say to Dr. Watson, "the game is afoot."

CHAPTER 4
TRUTH IS REVOLUTIONARY

No one knew from where he came. One day in April of 2006, he simply appeared, strolling down the cracked sidewalks of Main Street, the boarded up buildings seemingly a worthy compliment to his unkempt nature. He was moderately tall, comely, with a very irreverent countenance, such that those who saw him would respect him, but there was also an element of this man to fear, made plain by his assured manner of gliding wilfully down the nearly deserted street. His chestnut hair was long, curling and wavering about his shoulders. Although a bit scraggily, it glistened in the midday sun, almost seeming to shimmer like a diamond under a bright lit lamp. In the midst of his head was a seam, parting the hair slightly off centre to the left. His dark forehead was smooth except for some pock marks that seemed to be from scars made long ago. The thick, but trimmed, bearded face was without a spot or wrinkle. Appearing to be in his early 30's, his rather prominent nose seemed to bend slightly to the right. Moderately thick lips were parted enough to show glimmering white teeth that were slightly crooked on the bottom. Oh, but his gaze! His grey, clear, glinting, piercing eyes seemed courteous,but there was a tinge of redness within, almost as if they harboured some righteous indignation. In proportion, he was thin, but not emaciated-looking. Then, there were his hands. They seemed soft, but appeared to bear some calluses from years as a manual labourer. And on both his wrists were horrible pierced scars, apparently inflicted in some horrible accident.

The tiny hamlet of Woodbury Creek in southern New Jersey was about to witness events that would not just stir up this small, out-of-the-way spot on the vast planet called earth, but it would be the focal point for an earthquake of ideas that would rally the powerful and privileged in a corrupt society that feasted on propagandized manipulation of the masses to worship at the altar of greed. The seemingly innocuous events around Woodbury Creek would rally the forces of evil to squelch the stirrings of revolution that might crumble their empire that was based on deceit.

At the end of the street, he stopped in the park near the babbling creek that gave the town its name. Leaning against an elm tree that was just starting to awaken from the winter dormant stage, he started conversing with a group of youngsters who had gathered around, attracted, no doubt, by the charismatic nature of this tall, thin, dark-skinned, imposing figure of a man.

There was only obligatory small talk, but as the mid-day Saturday sun brightened, burning away the clouds, his chestnut hair and beard seemed to give off glistening rays, appearing to create a celestial appearance. Never had mankind seen a greater, sweeter, more serene countenance. As the adults in the park meandered over to listen to him speak of a new day for those who were willing to demand their rights as members of the human race, they all seemed mesmerized by his soft, gentle oratory. Saying there was no such thing as sedition or rebellion when done in pursuit of justice for those who were relegated to a life of want by the rich barons of greed, the adults seemed mesmerized with every word, almost as in a trance. The children from about 11 to 14, who had originally gathered around him, were equally enthralled, seeming to understand the intricacies of the machinations of woe which he was spinning.

The local sheriff was walking through the park, and noticing the crowd, meandered over to see what was going on. Looking at the sheriff, the comely orator smiled and said, "we have among us the law. That is the law as we know it, but there is no law as long as those with authority refuse to protect the weak from the strong who prey on those of us left to forage for daily sustenance in

28

the offices, factories, shops and fields of despair that are used by the wealthy and powerful to keep us in bondage to them."

Just as the sheriff was about to say something, his lips froze and his feet seemed fastened to the ground. He actually trembled in every limb, realizing that he was a guilty culprit of servitude to those who used him as a vassal for control of the populace. The sheriff stood in awe, as the tall stranger decried those in authority who dared suppress the masses who were crying for fairness and justice while being raped by an uncaring society run by and for the entitled classes.

The sheriff wanted to find him repelling but could not. This was an extraordinary man. There was nothing in him that was repelling, not in his character or in the words he spoke. Yet, the sheriff knew this was a man with whom he would have to reckon. This was a man who could stir up the populace. This man's magnetic simplicity and calm demeanour made him a threat. Sheriff Daniel Dillon knew there was trouble brewing. This man seemed capable of calming stormy seas with the mere wave of a hand, but what bothered Sheriff Dillon was that he also appeared capable of causing a storm. Yes, this man could indeed bring a raging tempest to Woodbury Creek.

The sheriff could not arrest a man for what he was saying, or could he? After all, this was America post 9/11, where what you said could get you locked-up for seditious intent. Everyone in America was suspect now. If you did not wear your American flag lapel pin, if you questioned your government, if you dared disagree with the wars of retribution against those who defied the USA, or if you were not sufficiently patriotic, you were an enemy of the state. This man was talking sedition. He was suggesting that people should question authority.

Finally, getting his feet to move, Sheriff Dillon walked toward the man and said, "fellow, you need to move-on. You are causing a disturbance."

The man very calmly replied, "it is not I who is causing the disturbance. It is you, and those like you, who do the bidding of the entitled classes that rule with the iron fist of repression."

Sheriff Dillon replied in a stern voice. "Just who the hell are you?"

The man smiled, raised his right hand with the index finger pointed skyward and said, "who am I? I am the one who is going to reach out with compassion to those marginalized by the powerful

30

evil minions of exploitation who sit in their gated, palatial monuments to greed and instruct people like you to keep us in bondage. But I am not going to teach them to be meek and turn the other cheek. I shall teach them the way of rebellion, rebellion against those who oppress us in the name of a system that takes from the many to reward the few. I have no fear of you or anyone else, because I am the son of man. If you want to be one who defends freedom, rather than sustain our bondage, throw your gun to the ground, fling your badge into the creek, and join your fellow sojourners in the search for salvation offered by the great father who has sent me again to offer hope to all those willing to embrace me and fight injustice."

The sheriff was dumbfounded by the calm demeanour maintained by this stranger. Yet, he knew that he was now forced into a situation that demanded action, as the crowd was obviously waiting to see which one would back down.

Walking to the sheriff, the man put his hand on his shoulder, slightly turned him toward the river and pointed at the babbling water. "That water is like me. It is calm, serene and patient. Yet, further down the stream, there might be rapids where the water will pick up speed and energy. Do not mistake a person's meekness for weakness. Please

31

remember that the gentle animal when cornered will fight furiously for survival. Be careful that you do not corner the meek and fearful among us, for even they have the instinct of survival, and the time is near when survival will require rebellion."

The sheriff lowered his head and walked away. The stranger turned toward the crowd that was growing larger, and now numbered at least 100. Raising both his hands toward the sky, he said, "he goes from us, because he cannot justify our repression at the moment. However, know that those who control him will not tolerate me for long. We, who speak out against conformity; we, who refuse to bend to conventionality; we, who demand social justice in a society that has none; we will be locked up in the gulags for refusing to play by the rules imposed by the privileged and powerful. Make no mistake that you live in a society with 5% of the world's population, but 25% of the world's prisoners languishing in jails to protect society from those deemed a threat. Do you really believe all who are locked away behind the iron bars of cruelty are there because of quilt. Yes, many are, but many are also there because they are simply guilty of questioning authority. Prisons are an abomination where many of the marginalized in this society are incarcerated, not to protect society, but to protect a system of

32

of economic and political servitude."

The crowd was hanging on every word that poured forth from this enlightened man. Not speaking for at least a minute, he still held the crowd spellbound by his mere presence. Then he stepped onto a picnic table so all could see him better. The crowd grew larger as word spread about the spell-binding orator who was revelling the people with stories. In a town of only 2000 people, the park now swelled to at least 500 eager individuals, waiting for the next pearl of wisdom to roll from the lips of the stranger.

Among the crowd was a man named Dixon Long, a private detective from Arkansas, who had been in Woodbury Creek to deliver a valuable package to a local banker. After delivering the package, he noticed a crowd gathering in the park across the street from the bank. His inquisitive nature dictated that he find out what was going on. Mingling with the crowd, he was awe-struck by this tall, dark, scraggily-glad stranger. The sun's rays seemed to dance about his head, giving off a celestial glow. When the stranger raised his hands to emphasize a point, the deep scars on his wrists gleamed, almost as if a huge spike had been driven through them. When the gentle breeze would blow his chestnut hair above his forehead, you

33

could see some symmetrical indentations, almost as if his skin at been pricked by thorns.

Standing beside a young woman, Dixon asked her who was this strange person. The woman simply said, "I do not know. Yet, I seem to have known him forever. He is meek, yet powerful. Listen, listen to his words of wisdom."

Taking a spiral notebook from the small bag he was carrying and looking at it occasionally for a reminder of what he wanted to say, the stranger began a series of parables.

"Listen my friends to words that will plant a seed in each of you. It is a seed that will grow into a mighty tree that will spread its branches and provide shade for the weary in a country that is filled with those who need a canopy of hope from the mighty tree of life. Today, I plant the seed, tomorrow some of you will become towering trees, while others will tarry, not water the seed and stand idly by as it wilts and dies from neglect. As always, the choice is yours. Remember that from a few seeds, a thick, lush forest can be born that will soar into the heavens."

Dixon moved forward through the crowd to get closer to the orator. Each step seemed to bring him more peace and tranquility. It was as if he began to soar above the crowd on the words of this man with piercing, peaceful eyes. Yes, the eyes, the eyes were the window to this man's soul and there was serenity in them. Words could lie. Politicians and business tycoons proved that every day, but the eyes of this man made you feel that he spoke from the heart. Words without feelings carried no solace to the weary. This man felt deeply about humanity and the plight of those who toiled in the fields of despair in a land of broken dreams where the mighty ruled unchallenged. Who was this man?

As Dixon finally made it to the front of the crowd, the man looked down at him and with sereneness said, "this man seeks the peace that only comes from within. He is drawn to me like all of you here today, but I can promise you that many of you will not heed my cries to stop your slumber and rise like sleeping lions in search of their prey. Most of you will refuse to stand against the tyranny that enslaves you. I am not here to tell you to meekly accept your fate. I have returned many times in many places, but my message has been subverted by those who want to enslave you. Remember that I am a revolutionary, and that I am not only the true son of God, I am the SON OF THUNDER."

35

As the Son of Thunder

The sky was cloudless, but as he uttered those words, the mighty rumbling sound of thunder roared in the distance and the sun's rays danced about his head, giving off a translucent glow.

Many in the crowd stood in awe, but others were unimpressed by those words or the sound of thunder on a cloudless day. Several pointed toward the factory in the distance, as if to say the sound came from there.

Suddenly, a deafening silence spread through the crowd. The silence was over-powering, as the crowd suddenly realized what this man was saying. He was claiming to be the son of God. Then, a voice from the back shouted, "you fraud, how dare you claim to be Jesus."

Unbowed and defiant, the man replied, "yes, my name is Jesus, as given to me by my blessed mother. You, who doubt me will sit smugly in your church pews on Sunday and listen to the many pontificators of judgmental arrogance disgrace my name by ascribing to me that which is an abomination in my eyes, because you have turned your hearts and minds over to those who purvey deceit. The New Testament that you read has been altered many times by scribes who were told by the church leaders what had to be written."

36

"Those leaders hijacked the real truth and subverted it to serve their own narrow, selfish interests. I am here to tell the truth, and let you decide for yourself what must be done to please the son-of-man. Be assured that I am not the meek man who turned the other cheek. I am the man who saw evil and confronted it. I am the man who refused to bow before tyranny. I went to my death many times, in many ways, in many different places, always bewildered by those who profess to love and honour me, but betray all for which I stand."

As many in the crowd drifted away, shaking their heads in disbelief that the tall, thin stranger had the nerve to say he was Jesus, Dixon Long stood still. Mesmerized by this charismatic man, he awaited the next words of wisdom from a man whom he held in awe.

"I do not blame those who turn their backs on me. They are all victims of a cruel system that binds them in chains they cannot see. Most of you think you live in the land of the free, but do not realize that unless you have wealth or power, there is no freedom in a land that refuses to reach out with the hand of compassion to truly create equal opportunity for all. Is the child born to a poor woman in the ghettos of despair equal to the child

37

born to a woman from the gated enclaves of the walled-off rich?"

"I am not here to go meekly into the night. I am here to do as I always have. I want to arouse all of you to fight for justice, just as I did in ancient Israel. I am a man of compassion, but I am also a man who sees the corrupt nature of the world as it has evolved into a corporate and religious theocracy that enslaves all of humanity to the most insidious disease to ever ravage the earth. That disease is greed, and greed is a part of all I survey in this land of broken dreams and promises. And this virus has spread across the world like a plague, destroying all hope for a just world that is filled with everything needed for humanity, if only those who control it would share their bounty with the unfortunate."

Looking out at the approximately 200 who remained, the man claiming to be Jesus looked down at Dixon Long, smiled and continued. "All of you come back here tomorrow at the same time, and I shall share some parables with you that will show all of you the way to end your enslavement. Go home, talk about what I have said, and spread the word that one who speaks the truth is at hand and offers deliverance to those willing to fight for the justice that is due us all."

38

As he started to step down from the picnic table that had served as his oratorical dais, he halted, looked out at the crowd and said, "I shall be among you for awhile, but be assured that like always, I will be betrayed and turned over to those who fear my words and these people will again put me to death. Too many minds have been manipulated by the pontificators of hate who use my name to enslave billions. Those who truly love justice will always stand with me against the evil of tyrants who wrap all of you in bondage to greed and judgemental arrogance. I have suffered mightily because in the face of deceit, truth becomes revolutionary."

CHAPTER 5
SOCIAL AND ECONOMIC JUSTICE

Arriving in New York, Aaron left the airport and found himself constantly glancing behind to see if he was being followed. The cab driver was really chatty, but the usually jovial Aaron was concerned about matters that kept him in deep thought.

He kept mulling over the events of the past two days. What was the government up to this time? Long ago, while in the military, Aaron had learned that the government was a lie-factory that churned out subterfuge like crap through a goose to keep the American public in line. Most people were too wrapped up in petty things, like who would be the next American Idol, to realize that they were all a pack of sheep that were being led to the slaughter by the government and its corporate masters. Aaron had killed two FBI agents, and there was not a word about it in the papers. The big cover-up was in full swing, but how long would it take them to finger him and send out the government goon squads to silence him. Silence him about what, though? What did he know? All he had done was visit an old friend who told him about a mystical man who showed up in New Jersey in 2006. What was the FBI looking for, and why did they come in with guns blazing?

40

As the cab pulled up at his office, he looked down in the seat and saw the answer. That was it. The FBI was after the spiral notebook. That was the key to the whole thing. But why had they killed Dixon? What was the purpose of killing a man for a spiral notebook?

Aaron paid the cabby, grabbed the spiral notebook and quickly exited the cab. As he approached the revolving doors of the Kaiser Building, a new neighbourhood derelict, pushing her shopping cart, said, "hello stranger. Got some change for a poor old woman?"

Not having time to engage in his usual banter with the derelicts of the area, Aaron quickly reached in his pocket and handed her all his change, as he continued through the revolving doors into the building.

Poor old woman, just another one of the many who had been tossed aside by a system that criminalized poverty. In a city filled with affluence, the marginalized were constantly increasing as they were tossed aside by a society that could always find money for bombs and bullets, but never find the money to reach out with the hand of compassion to those who had been trampled on by an uncaring economic system.

41

Well, Aaron would have to contemplate the folly of people like the shopping cart lady another time. Right now, he had to face his own folly. Killing two FBI agents, even in self-defence, was not something that could go unpunished by a government that made sure people respected the law by making them fear it. Give someone a position of authority and they thought they had carte blanche to ride rough-shod over the citizens who were constantly told how free they were, but were, in fact, nothing but whimpering wimps expected to cow-tow to the patriotic flag-waving propaganda that had imprisoned them all into economic servitude. Fear was the key element in control: fear of manufactured enemies, fear of financial ruin, fear of government, fear of God, fear of the wealthy and powerful. Well, Aaron was not the average American Joe who quivered in timid solicitude before the behemoths of the all-powerful evil of capitalism. He was one citizen who would go down fighting, kicking, clawing and spewing the last bullets in his gun to defend the sanctity of his personal freedom that would never be turned over to the hypocritical, arrogant, self-serving, moneyed oligarchy that ruled the American nation with iron-fisted brutality. Aaron Adams was a dying breed, a real freedom-loving American who had not fallen victim to the propaganda spewed out by the purveyors of deceit.

42

His second floor office was a small suite with an attached bedroom that served as an apartment. His work was his life, so it made perfect sense to live where he worked. He had once had a secretary, but lost her in the case of the apocalyptic box that made him the most famous private-eye in all of America. That had been almost 30 years ago, and ever since his life had been on a down-hill spiral as he not only lost his secretary, but the love of his life. Nothing really mattered to him after that. Each day was just a journey down a boulevard of broken dreams, but he still managed to survive, but that is all his life was, just survival.

He had been buoyed by the call from Dixon, a friend he had not seen in almost 10 years, but the camaraderie they shared in the jungles of Vietnam had made them eternally bound together. They had survived the evil of an unjust war that had taught them both how corrupt and evil the system of patriotic servitude was. For a short time, they shared a professional relationship as partners in a detective agency, but Dixon longed to return to his native Arkansas and a more sublime existence. Yet, their bond was never broken. Those who fight together to survive forge a strong bond that time and distance can never put asunder. Now, Dixon was also gone, and Aaron would not rest until the perpetrators of the carnage in Little Rock were discovered and made to pay for their acts, not by a government that turned a blind eye to evil acts of its minions, but by Aaron Adams, who could deal out justice from the barrel of his big bastard of a 45.

He settled in behind the old oak desk, propped up his feet, leaned back in the chair and thought back on the events of the past two days. There was nowhere he could turn for help. All governments were run by self-serving politicians whose only goal was getting what they could for themselves, their families and their cronies. Only the rich and powerful were accorded justice, if you could call it that, in a country where the average Joe was always on the outside looking in. Aaron had no power, no wealth and frankly didn't want either. He was a truly free man, whose disdain for authority had made him a pariah with those in power, because he saw through their façade. Aaron had no respect for them and what they represented.

Aaron owed Dixon, and he knew the only way to repay him was to do what he asked. Tomorrow, he would go to Woodbury Creek and seek out information on the stranger who was calling himself Jesus.

44

Dixon had not lived to tell him the entire story, but Aaron was committed now to at least seek out this man who had captivated Dixon and apparently so enraged the authorities that for some reason, they had dispatched the F.B.I. to eliminate Dixon and retrieve the spiral binder that was a precursor of trouble.

Looking out his window at the derelict woman who had parked her shopping cart at an angle against the building and curled up in a tight ball under Aaron's window, he thought about how so many others were like her, their entire belongings setting in a shopping cart. Now, the corporations that created the situations that institutionalized poverty were installing shopping carts that required payment to remove them from a queue. That way, they could protect their property from the poor who needed them for survival. Aaron thought that one day he would simply put in coins and have the derelicts line up and go off with the carts from a corporate owned grocery store. What capitalistic arrogance? The corporations thought making you put in a quarter would keep you from stealing a cart. Inconvenience their customers, so they can prevent the theft of a shopping cart. Greed was so rampant that it was the real religion in America, and there was no stopping it, because the populace had been brainwashed into believing

45

that the pursuit of wealth was an enviable trait. Now, a man calling himself Jesus had shown up and was probably deriding the loss of compassion. That was revolutionary alright, preaching compassion in a nation that turned its back on the needy while rewarding the rich and powerful. Tomorrow, Aaron would find out more about this man, and why Dixon Long had been targeted by the F.B.I.

Looking at the spiral notebook on his desk, he knew that it had to be hidden in case anyone showed up looking for it. Why would anyone want it, anyway? It was simply a bunch of gibberish prose written by an obviously deranged man who claimed to be Lord Jesus Christ. Hell, he was probably just another manipulative son-of-bitch who wanted to hoodwink a pack of religious nuts into forking over their life-savings to follow him to the promised land. Meanwhile, as his followers were waiting for the rapture, he would be enjoying the high-life. The world was full of false messiahs and even more full of idiots who would follow them. Yet, the notebook meant something to Dixon, and that was reason enough to assure its safety.

There was an old safe in the wall, but that would be easy for even an amateur to get into. And one

As the Son of Thunder

thing Aaron knew about the F.B.I., they were not amateurs. From the beginning, J. Edgar Hoover had made the F.B.I. into a professional organization dedicated to protecting America from the insidious evil of those who dared question authority. The jails were full of people the F.B. I. had legitimately put there, but the jails were also full of people who had been railroaded by an organization that too often served the interests of the few at the expense of the many. From the socialists of the 1930's, to the communists of the 1950's, to the radicals of the 1960's, to the patriots who questioned the wars of conquest today, the F.B.I. had made sure that the government's interests were served while ignoring real justice.

Aaron looked down at the filled waste basket. He could not afford a cleaning service, so it often overflowed until he felt like walking down to the trash bin to empty it. He removed the notebook from his desk and placed it at the bottom of the trash can, being careful to make sure the trash on top of it looked like it was randomly disposed of.

Looking out the window at the derelict lady sleeping on the sidewalk, he drifted off to sleep wondering if there was a Jesus, what he would think of a rich country that refused to provide the poor with social and economic justice.

As the Son of Thunder

CHAPTER 6
FROM THE DARKNESS INTO THE LIGHT

That day in Woodbury Creek, when Jesus stepped down from the picnic table, he put his arms on Dixon's shoulder and said, "walk with me brother."

Dixon, mesmerized by the strong countenance of the man, could not reply. He just started walking out of the park with him. Walking in silence, Dixon felt at ease and at peace. This man was someone who did not need to speak in order to convey his affection. Yet, there was power, the power of conviction that made him seem formidable.

At the edge of the park, the man turned to Dixon and said, "you need to make a decision. You need to get busy living or get busy dying. You walk with me and you may die, but you will live as you have never lived before – free of fear and free of constraint by those who would make you a slave to the misery of a society based on greed. Like all my beloved children, you have a choice. You can stand with me and fight the tyranny of economic and social oppression, or you can worship at the feet of those I term Satan's mentally challenged brothers."

48

The man smiled, leaned forward and continued, "remember that death is the end for all of us, but that does not mean you die. Your body decays, but the ideas for which you stand will continue on forever. Nothing good ever really dies."

Dixon, perplexed and confused asked, "but why me?"

"But why not you my brother? I can look into your eyes and see deep within your soul. I see the goodness that makes you a true disciple of justice and truth. You are a good, kind and decent man. Have you not seen suffering and tried to heal it? Have you not seen the wrongs of a society based on greed and tried to right it? Have you not been in war and seen the folly of it? Are you not like me? Don't you see things as they are and ask why they must be that way? Do you not dream of things that never were and ask why things cannot change?"

Dixon, disconcerted by how this man seemed to know all about his inner most thoughts, could not answer.

The wise man smiled and said, "do not be bewildered by what I know about you. I can see things even you don't know about yourself."

As the Son of Thunder

Dixon, somewhat mystified, replied, "who are you, really?"

Again smiling, he replied as his twinkling eyes seemed to dance with glee, "I am whomever you want me to be. I am he who brings love to those who need it. I am he who reaches out with compassion to those who never receive it. I am he who demands little but gives a lot. I am he who can show all of those trapped in the pits of economic despair and who are denied simple human justice the path that will allow them to throw off their chains of bondage."

Turning to a strikingly beautiful woman with dark eyes and flowing black hair, who was walking alongside Dixon, he pointed directly at her and continued his soliloquy. "She wonders why she is following me? She cannot understand why she is drawn to me. She is what most would call a wanton woman. She makes her living by offering sexual favours to men, most of whom look with disdain on her, when, in fact, it is they for whom I have disdain. She survives in the best way she can, and I know there have been times when she gave her sexual favours for free to those who needed the warmth of another human being. She is a good woman who reaches out with compassion to those in despair. The real whores of

50

the world are those who go to church on Sunday, and throw a coin or two into the collection plate, which they think buys them favour with God. Then on Monday, they sit in their leather chairs behind mahogany desks where they take advantage of the less fortunate, all the time deriding those who are not right with God."

The woman could not understand how he knew all this about her. Bewildered, she replied, "how do you know this? My name is Mary Madison, and I have been a prostitute for 20 years, ever since I was 16. I do not know you. Yet, you even know that I do give my sexual favours away for free to a few older men. They visit me just to feel my body next to theirs, because they have lost the wives that they loved dearly. They just long for the warmth they miss. I feel good when I do this. Yet, I feel ashamed at the same time."

That all knowing smile crept across his lips again as his eyes gleamed with pleasure. "Why should you be ashamed. Compassion is at the root of whom we are as human beings. Nor should you be ashamed of your profession. Sex is nothing more than recreational activity between consenting adults. It is the purveyors of deceit who profess to speak for God who must be condemned.They point the finger of condemnation

51

while doing that which they condemn. I make no secret of the joy I receive from gazing at a beautiful woman, but I see the inner beauty of each woman. You are a most striking woman, who, no doubt, titillates the libido of all men who gaze upon you. Yet, the real beauty you bear shines brighter than that which is on the surface."

"Come Mary, walk with me and my new found friend," said Jesus as he gave a quizzical look at Dixon, like he was asking his name.

Dixon, now smiling himself, but wondering why he was so drawn to this charismatic man, replied, "Dixon."

The stragglers that were following Dixon, Mary and Jesus all begin to tell him their names, uttering them as if it would give them some type of anointed sanctity just to let him know who they were. At the end of the park, the man turned and said, "all of you go now and do not forget the few things I have taught you today. Be aware that each one of you has a choice to bow before tyranny or to stand like a rock against it. Those who stand against it may face death, but it is a death of a free man. Being truly free is something none of you really know, because you have accepted the fate foisted on you by authority. Know there is only

52

one authority to whom you must answer, your own conscience. Look deep within and ask yourself if you have served the good of mankind each day of your life. If the answer is yes, then you have earned your checkmark in the book of life."

Dixon Long and Mary Madison continued to walk with this wise sage through the boarded up downtown. Looking at the dilapidated buildings, Jesus said, "what a shame that a way of life that afforded people the opportunity to be in business for themselves has been abrogated by the corporate thugs who now control everything. There will never be any economic justice as long as corporations and their government lackeys continue to enslave the people of this country to an idea that died long ago. What a shame that people now line-up to be made slaves. How can you help people who cannot see their own chains?"

Dixon replied, "I think people are too stupid to understand that they have no freedom. They act as they are told without ever questioning authority. Thousands of advertisements every day showing you can only be happy by buying things, the asinine shows that pass as entertainment and the constant government and corporate propaganda

53

have turned everyone into a bunch of mindless robots perfectly willing to let someone else do their thinking for them."

Smiling, the man calling himself Jesus, replied, "my dear Dixon, that is why I was attracted to you. I could immediately see that you were a man who understood that those who do not question authority are nothing more than slaves."

Mary Madison interjected in a quiet demure way, "so, you do not believe as the Bible says that we should render unto Caesar what is Caesar's?"

"Mary, I know the Bible, and I know that it is an abomination of what I stand for in a world that is filled with cruelty of the vilest form. The Bible sanctions slavery. The Bible says you can sell your daughter to the highest bidder. The Bible says you can kill a rebellious son? The Bible is filled with cruelty which does not represent what my heavenly father really stands for. It is filled with deceit promulgated by those who want supplication and fear from all humanity but the chosen few who hold the reins of power and wealth. Why would Caesar be rendered anything? He was an evil conqueror. Those who have much should share their bounty with those who have little. If a coin bears the image of Caesar does it

54

As the Son of Thunder

belong to Caesar or to the one who earned it with his labour? Caesar earned nothing. He made other soldiers earn it for him with their blood. His image is on that coin because he shed the blood of many to benefit the few. Today, the worship of wealth has made slaves out of 99% of the world to benefit the 1% who think they are the privileged class and should not share their bounty. The wealthy and powerful today are like Caesar, manipulating others for self-aggrandizement."

Dixon, enthralled by the perceptive nature of his new found friend, chimed in, "what are we to do then?"

"You are to listen intently to what I say. I shall show you the way to end the misery of mankind. It is not the meek way you have been taught, because being meek only plays into the hands of the oppressors. Was it Martin Luther King and his non-violent eloquence that got the U.S. government to attack racism, or was it the Black Panthers and their brethren in the ghettos of despair who started burning down the cities of America? Was it the meek working people with cup in hand begging for a scrap of bread from the captains of industry who created a modicum of fairness in the workplace, or was it the union rebels who started destroying the factories where

As the Son of Thunder

they toiled for menial wages while the robber barons lived lives of excess? When Fidel Castro tried to overturn the tyranny of the oppressors without a gun, he was defeated, but when he took up the gun to eradicate the evil, he was victorious. When Che Guevara was a doctor in Argentina, he helped a few people, but when he became a revolutionary, he helped millions. Make no mistake, turning the other cheek gets you slapped by those who have no compassion. There is a time to turn the other cheek, but when dealing with those who are determined to keep you in chains, turning the other cheek will only get you more chains."

A group of stragglers gathered closer around Mary, Dixon and Jesus. Again, the people were drawn to the power of this charismatic man's words and the quiet eloquence from a voice that was soft but still resonated with the power of a raging storm heading for the quiet shore of a deserted beach. You could see that this man was revelling in his power to captivate a few souls with his wisdom. Yet, he was not prideful, just grateful for the interest showed by the few who had gathered around him.

Someone in the back of the crowd shouted, "are you running for some political office?"

As the Son of Thunder

Smiling, Jesus replied, "this nation is filled with politicians who make lies sound like truth and the murder of innocents abroad seem justifiable in the name of national security. Politicians are the lowest form of humanity. They are elected to help the people, but only help themselves. They serve the interests of the few at the expense of the many. I am running for nothing. I am running from something. I am running from lies, deceit, pettiness, jealousy, injustice and institutionalized poverty. I want others to join me by turning their backs on these evils and standing up to those who trample on us with the jack-booted feet of economic and social oppression."

Pushing his way to the front of the crowd, an elderly man asked Jesus why he was preaching on the side of the street, and not on television where he could reach a bigger audience.

Looking at the man with a calm demeanour, he replied, "I am not preaching on television, because all those who stoop to selling me like a tube of toothpaste do not offer anyone salvation. They only demean me and themselves by reducing the love of God to a commodity to be peddled like any other product in a society where one's worth is judged by what is in their bank account, rather than by what they have in their heart."

57

As the crowd grew larger, Jesus began to walk down the street, heading out of town. The people followed, straining to get nearer to him. Yet, no matter how far they were from him, they felt his warmth radiate all about them.

A teenage Native American child, tugging the arm of his mother, made his way to Jesus' side. Looking up at the somewhat frail but powerful looking man, he asked, "my people have suffered mightily at the hands of the government. How can we get justice where there is none?"

Jesus, never breaking stride, raised his voice so all could hear. "Geronimo, Sitting Bull, Crazy Horse, Red Cloud, Gall, Leonard Peltier and countless others tried to get justice for their people from the white oppressors. They were all jailed or killed for daring to question the authority of the white government. The pursuit of justice is fraught with danger. You must be willing to pay the supreme price to achieve it. It cannot be achieved by complacency. The complacent only receive the back hand of the oppressor. Unfortunately, a million Native Americans marching on Congress have less power than one corporate lobbyist with a cheque book in his hand. Mao once said that power comes from the barrel of a gun. The government knows that, and they arm themselves

58

and put thugs in uniforms to keep the people in check. When government becomes too oppressive, the time honoured tradition is rebellion. A government that does not respect its people should receive no respect from the people. All power ultimately rests with the people, if the people are willing to use the power. A gun can extinguish a life, but it cannot extinguish an idea. Think about what I have said, my son, and one day your people, allied with all the oppressed of the world, may free yourselves from bondage."

The man calling himself Jesus, lifted his right hand toward the sky. He pointed his index finger toward the sitting sun and said, "another day fades, but believe me, I offer you the sunshine of a brighter day tomorrow. I shall be in the park early in the day. Join me, and I shall share with you the means to free yourself from the bondage that has you in its grip and is squeezing the very life out of you."

As the crowd broke-up, Jesus turned to Mary and Dixon. "So, which one of you is going to offer me a bed for the night?"

Mary interjected, "I have a small apartment down the street where I turn tricks. I am afraid you would find my work habits offensive."

As the Son of Thunder

With a mindful, warm, compassionate smile; the tall, thin man said in his soft, melodious voice, "you do what society forces you to do in order to survive. Anyone who judges you is condemning themselves. Why would I judge you? Do you pollute the environment for monetary gain? Do you steal from widows who cannot make their rent or mortgage payments? Do you corrupt the youth with encouragement to practice materialism? Do you lie to get people to support unjust wars? Do you preach morality and then do the very thing you define as immoral? Which is a greater sin, sexual promiscuity for monetary rewards, or sanctioning an unjust system of economic servitude? You are not a sinner. It is those who call you sinner who are an abomination."

Dixon, realizing he had a plane to catch, said, "I am due back in Little Rock tomorrow, so I have no place to stay myself, but I will gladly get a motel room for you. However, I really must leave now."

Jesus smiled and said, "Your business is here right now Dixon, as is Mary's. The business I have to offer is more important than what awaits you in Arkansas. I am going to let you be the conduit for a story that must be told. The next few days, before the day of my sacrifice, I shall lay out the map of true redemption for those who will listen. Most will turn their backs on me, while a few, who yearn to be truly free and escape the calamity of modern slavery, will sow the seeds of rebellion. Make no mistake, I shall be sacrificed at the altar of the wicked who can not tolerate my rebellious message that might inflame those who are in bondage. Come, let's share Mary's humble abode, for tomorrow will be a busy day for us all."

Turning, taking Mary by the hand, and nodding his head up and down at Dixon, it was almost as if, in his quiet determined manner, he was ordering them to do as he wanted. As they walked silently toward Mary's apartment, the sun disappeared below the horizon and they were all bathed in an eerie darkness that seemed to wrap itself around them like a blanket. A chilly wind blew from the west and lightly tussled the chestnut hair of this imposing man as he said, "come now and walk with me from the darkness into the light."

61

CHAPTER 7
HE IS DANGEROUS

The next morning, Dixon and Jesus got up around 6:00 AM, as they had shared Mary's bed while she slept in the living room on the sofa. She had entertained one man that evening, but turned down another who came by late, because she felt a great uneasiness about having a sexual rendezvous, in spite of the non-judgemental nature of the tall, thin stranger.

Putting on rumbled clothing, Jesus asked Dixon if he would buy him some clothes, as he had none with him and no money. All three got in Dixon's rental car, had breakfast and then headed to the nearby town of Woodbury to the Wal-Mart that opened at 8:00 AM, where the tall, thin man calling himself Jesus, was careful to buy the cheapest two pairs of slacks, some underwear and four shirts. As they were checking out, a lady, obviously in her 70's, looked quizzically at the man calling himself Jesus.

Jesus reached out and touched her hand as she was putting the merchandise in a large bag. Her face lit up and it was obvious that she wanted to say something to him, but could not find the words. It was he, who, with his soft, melodic voice uttered the words she could not, "yes, I am he who understands your plight. It is disconcerting to live in a society where you have to toil at your age, because those with power refuse to make your life all it should be after years of struggle. I can only offer you my heartfelt love, and assure you that your sacrifices will be long remembered by those you cared for over the years. Your sacrifices have been recorded in the book of life, and your goodness will forever dwell in the lives of others you have touched."

Concerned about the slow-up in the check-out line, a manager made his way to the checkers' cash register and said, "is there a problem here?"

Jesus, looking directly at the manager replied, "the problem is all around you in this monument to greed, but you are too blind to see it."

As he picked up the bag, he motioned with his right index finger for Mary and Dixon to leave. The cashier simply said, "thank you for your love."

Jesus looked over his shoulder as he continued to walk away and said, "it is I who should thank you for your love, and the love of all who toil in places of bondage like this."

63

The manager, dumbfounded, could not utter a word, as he watched the tall stranger walk away. Mary and Dixon smiled at each other, knowing that this man was capable of a love like they had never seen before.

Back at Mary's apartment, the three had a leisurely morning as they bathed and got ready for what the tall stranger called an eventful day of discovery.

When Dixon reiterated his need to return to Little Rock, Jesus counselled him to not tarry if he indeed thought the business of making money was more important than the business of lifting up humanity from the abyss of misery promulgated by a corrupt and evil society bent on the subjugation of all to the culture of greed.

Dixon, always an abject anti-capitalist who pursued a living, but not wealth, replied, "you misjudge me. I only want what it takes to survive in a society where there is no compassion for those who fall through the cracks of an economic system that requires devotion to self-interest."

Reaching out with his right hand and touching Dixon on the shoulder, Jesus said, "but, I am going to show you how to lift up those who fall

64

between the cracks. Walk with me for a few days, and you may suffer from those who fear me and my message, but you will live as you have never lived before, secure in the knowledge that you have reached out with tenderness and mercy to those relegated to serve the masters of deceit in this corrupt, vile society that equates Christianity with the greed that is proclaimed an enviable trait for mankind. I cannot guarantee that you will not pay the supreme sacrifice for devotion to me, but I can assure you that any sacrifice for the sanctity of mankind, is a sacrifice worth making."

Dixon noticed a smile creep across Jesus' face as he replied, "my business can wait."

Jesus, looking at Dixon, then at Mary, said, "but mine cannot wait. Come, let us sow some seeds of dissent today. Let's agitate and unnerve those who would make us all slaves to the evil of complacency."

Stopping for lunch at the only restaurant downtown, the three sit in a booth near a window. In the booth behind them were three well dressed patrons. One was obviously a minister based upon the clergy collar he wore. The other most likely a businessman, as he wore what appeared to be a well-tailored, expensive suit, and the third was an immaculately attired haughty-looking woman of about 50.

Jesus' back was to their booth, but as he and his friends were finishing their sandwiches, he overheard the minister say, "there is that Jezebel who fornicates with married men and charges for her pleasures. In the old days, when this nation enforced a code of morality, she would be run out of town."

The businessman chortled, "yeah, and the people who associate with her should be run out of town, too."

The woman sitting behind Jesus actually turned her head, stared at Mary for a brief second, turned back to her companions and said, "it is disgusting that she has the nerve to show her face in public."

Jesus, in his measured, calm tone of voice, turned around and addressed the three. "First, my dear man, you wear an ecclesiastical collar that should indicate you judge not, least you be judged. Secondly, you point the finger of condemnation at this woman, when the real culprits are those who avail themselves of her services while lying to their wives. And in some cases, the men who use her services may be in search of the warmth that is

66

not available to them at home."

Looking at the businessman, Jesus was more direct. "And what is your profession sir?"

Indignantly, the man replied, "I am a banker."

Jesus looked him directly in the eyes, and without any hesitation said, "you have the nerve to condemn her? She fornicates for pocket change. You sir, fuck people every day in a much more insidious way. You screw widows, orphans and the poor out of their hard earned money. You reward yourself with huge bonuses while decrying those who beg for a crumb from your table of plenty."

Looking down at the woman, Jesus continued. "And you madam, how many times have you been taken out to dinner, a movie or a cultural event by a man and rewarded your escort with sex. Are you any different than this woman you demean? You, madam, are much worse than she. You think she is beneath you. Believe me, I, the son of man, have much more contempt for you than I have for her. You condemn, she does not."

The three stared at Jesus, dumbfounded and bewildered by the nerve of the stranger.

67

Mary, standing by the booth, aghast at the boldness of her new found friend, took his arm, smiled and proudly walked out the door with him. They could hear the mumbling noises of people in the restaurant as the patrons were all discussing the grit of this man.

The minister looked at his friends and said, "the arrogance of that man, indeed. Who does he think he is? That man is crazy. He is dangerous, a menace to society."

Many in the restaurant nodded their heads in agreement with the minister, but a few had a quizzical look on their faces. And an even smaller number of people actually started to think about what this tall, scraggily haired stranger had said. Was this man right? Was it time to stop condemning and start embracing?

As they proceeded down Main Street, Dixon and Mary could not help but feel a certain pride in being beside this tower of strength. Although Jesus was slight in frame, somewhat unkempt, had a prominent nose, and highly visible scars about his forehead; he had an air about him that presented an imposing figure of a man. He seemed to exude self-confidence in a quiet, subdued fashion that demanded respect.

68

Coming out of his office as the three walked down the street, Sheriff Dillon walked in front of them, blocking their path. Looking directly at Jesus he said, "are you planning another day of rebel rousing in the park?"

The three came to a halt and Jesus replied, "Sheriff, you think teaching people to question authority is rebel rousing? You think it inappropriate to encourage people to get off their knees and demand social justice for themselves and their loved ones? Is it rebel rousing to point out that authorities like you represent the oppressors who enslave us all, as you enforce unjust laws promulgated by those who keep us in bondage? Is it unfitting to say that an eye for an eye and a tooth for a tooth is the revengeful prescription for perceived justice rather than real justice? Is it wrong to teach that the eyes are the lamp of the body, and if your eyes are dark, then so shall be your heart? You, sir, are at a crossroads. You can walk with me into the light, and brighten your eyes with the truth, or you can continue your journey in darkness that hardens your heart like all who refuse to reach out with understanding, love and compassion in a world where it is in short supply. I speak not about eternal life in the hereafter but of a meaningful life here and now."

69

The sheriff, unmoved but still in awe of this man replied, "I will have my eye on you, so watch your step."

Jesus, unnerved, walked away with his companions as he replied, "and I shall have my eye on you."

Once in the park, Jesus sit atop a picnic table with his feet resting on the attached bench. As people began to gather around to hear him, he instinctively stood up. The crowd grew to about one hundred, when one man standing in the back shouted, "if you are who you say you are, perform a miracle."

Jesus smiled and replied, "I am performing a miracle right now. It is a miracle that I am still able to stand here and speak, because you live in a country where it is seditious to speak the truth and to stand against the tyranny of the government. Be assured that the time is near when I shall be betrayed as I am always betrayed. Those who fear my message think they can extinguish it by extinguishing me. But killing me will never extinguish the ideas for which I stand. Those ideas shall live forever.

The man retorted, "so are the Bible miracles true

or all lies?"

Unperturbed, Jesus replied, "my friend, did you not give up believing in fairy tales when you were a child? Remember, the ancient people were like uneducated children, and could be easily convinced of things we would consider absurd today. It is said by those who want to control you that the Bible is the dictated word of God, but it was men who wrote it, even if God did dictate it. Do you not believe that a man can alter the word of God after all these years? Those of you who allow pompous, self-righteous purveyors of deceit to interpret God's word for you are nothing more than mindless sheep dependent on a Shepard to guide you. You follow the Shepard, even if he leads you off a cliff. You do not need a Bible to know the difference between right and wrong. That is in your heart, not a book."

The man, now becoming agitated, shouted, "so are you saying the miracles in the Bible are lies?"

Jesus, warming to the verbal sparring replied, "sir, are you simple minded enough to think that God brought down the walls of Jericho? Or, as a learned man, do you know something about acoustics, and realize that a thousand horns blaring in the wilderness can create sound vibrations that

71

could cause sandstone walls to crumble? There is generally a plausible explanation for any so-called miracle. God need not make miracles, all he need do is provide man with a brain, so that man can make his own miracles."

Many in the crowd shook their heads in agreement. The questioner, with a quizzical look on his face, was now contemplating what Jesus had said.

As the crowd steadily grew larger, several ministers who had been rounded up by the minister from the restaurant to see the arrogance of this man, pushed their way forward as people respectfully stepped aside in deference to their positions as clergy.

Looking down at these bastions of probity, Jesus pointed his right index finger at them and said, "why do you part for these men? Why are they so special that you would show them any more respect than the others in the crowd? Remember that you are all equal in my eyes. There is none who is exalted more than any other before my throne, because my throne is a picnic table or anywhere else that men hunger for justice. These men pontificate from luxurious churches that are supposed to be dedicated to the glory of God, but

72

would a loving God really want a magnificent edifice that is closed at night, when it could be opened so those without shelter could sleep in the pews? Churches are giant monuments to man's greed rather than his compassion. Do you not think God is appalled by those who sit in pews on Sundays to glorify themselves rather than God?"

One of the ministers shouted, "you are an abomination."

Smiling broadly and looking directly at the man, Jesus replied, "it is not I or my words that are abominable. It is the culture of greed that is an abomination. For as I have said before, your heart will always be where your riches are."

Taken aback, the minister turned to his colleagues and shrugged his shoulders, seemingly admitting that Jesus was certainly right about the scripture in regards to riches as quoted in Matthew.

Another minister bellowed loudly, "God does not begrudge us having things. We live in a wealthy country, where the right to have the comforts of life is available to each and everyone of us, if we are willing to work for them. You do not have to be poor to be a Christian."

73

Not missing a beat, Jesus replied, "you cannot serve both God and money. God has given enough for all men to be rich – rich in food by being able to plough the earth or fish the sea. Rich in water by the streams that abound. The problem is that a few men have decided that they, not God, should decide who owns the land and that it shall be tilled for profit rather than the sustenance of those who beg at the feet of the wealthy and powerful. Meanwhile, the church sanctions this evil, rather than fighting it. My church would stand against a system that allows a few to feast at the table of plenty while not even throwing a crumb to those in need. Be aware that this is evil of the vilest form, and this evil is not put there by the devil. It is put there by men. There is no devil, other than the devil of avaricious greed that rewards the few at the expense of the many."

The crowd, now grown to at least 300, roared with applause as Jesus stepped down from the table, took the arm of Mary and walked away with her and Dixon toward the stream that ran through the park.

The ministers, all equally dumbfounded, stormed out of the park, and one was heard in a barely audible whisper to say, "something has to be done about this man. He is dangerous."

74

CHAPTER 8
TINGLE BETWEEN AN OLD MAN'S LEGS

After sleeping at his desk all night, Aaron woke up stiff and had to stretch the kinks out of his back and neck. At 60, he thought to himself, if only that stiffness was in the one place I need it. Having been sexually active with a variety of partners over the years, Aaron had never grown accustomed to the aging process between his legs.

Looking out the window, he noticed the derelict lady was pushing her cart toward the public fountain at the end of the street, probably to wash her face and start another day begging for scraps in a once vibrant city that had simply been turned into yet another of a long list of metropolises where the poor were nothing but a nuisance that littered the paths of the affluent.

As Aaron turned to head to the washroom, he noticed a neatly attired balding man come up to the derelict lady and seem to say something, then walk briskly away and get into a black sedan. As the car pulled away from the curb, Aaron observed that it was driven by a white-haired man of about 50. The derelict lady turned her shopping cart around and headed up the street toward Aaron's building. Appearing to be in her 50's, she had the

75

gait of a much younger woman. Aaron thought to himself that she could be much younger than she appeared, as a life of want made people age much quicker, and she was obviously living a life of want, along with millions of others in a society that gave those at the top all the benefits while ignoring those at the bottom. In America, poverty was treated like a disease. If you were poor, it was your fault. Yeah, like a child had a choice to whom to be born? The very assholes who ranted and raved against abortion were perfectly willing to let that un-aborted child die from poverty or lack of medical care, but they had to be born, because abortion was murder? Of course, abandonment to life on the streets or refusing to provide a child with healthcare was not murder.

Showering and changing clothes, Aaron prepared to do what Dixon had asked of him, but first, he was going to touch base with his friend on the NYPD, John Havoc. John would know what was going on in New Jersey, and could maybe run a few checks for Aaron before he headed to South Jersey.

On the way out of the building, the derelict lady almost ran into Aaron and said, "excuse me. I know who you are, lots of people know you. You're Aaron Adams."

Aaron replied, "and whom do I have the pleasure of addressing?"

The lady, smiling through pearly white teeth, except for two front uppers that were missing, said, "I am Annie, just Annie. People around here have taken to calling me Sidewalk Annie. I suppose because I am always here on the sidewalk, trying to hustle a buck. You need your office cleaned? I can do a really good job cheap."

Aaron, surveying Annie up and down, noticed that her clothes, although ragged, appeared to be fairly new and clean. They were torn in an almost symmetrical way. Looking at her face, he deduced that she could not be anywhere near 50, as there were no crows feet around her eyes, and her hair, obviously not dyed, contained no grey. There seemed to be an air of sophistication about her.

Reaching into his billfold and removing a 5 dollar bill, he handed it to her and said, "Annie, my place is a mess, but it is a mess that allows me to know where everything is, so I will pass on the cleaning job. Here is a five, buy yourself some breakfast, and maybe I will let you clean another time. I have to be going now.

Smiling, Annie replied, "cool."

77

John Havoc was a big man in his early 40's. He gave the appearance of a man who could hold his own against any brawler anywhere, anytime. His prominent nose looked like it had been broken a few times too many. His eyes were deep and there were perpetual circles under them. Yet, his rough looks belied a more sedate nature, but you knew from the aura about him that he was not a man with whom you wanted to mess.

As Aaron sauntered into his office, Havoc, in his deep, gravely voice said, "damn my soul, if it isn't New York's last real private eye. How you doing Aaron?"

"Not that well. I could use a favour."

"And I thought you were here for a social call on an old friend."

"Well, you can call it a social call that includes a little information."

Havoc smiling, because he knew Aaron only came by when he was fishing for something, replied, "information doesn't come cheap these days. Your government charges for everything, because it is broke. Just like you and me, it is always on the abyss,except for the politicians with their outlandish salaries and parsimonious benefits."

Aaron surprised at Havoc's vocabulary replied, "where did you learn big words like parsimonious?"

"Hey, not all civil servants are dumb. Some of us study the Thesaurus on our two hour lunches."

Aaron, enjoying the banter, but realizing he was a man with limited time, because eventually he would have to deal with the F.B.I., cut to the chase. "Well, I may take you out on one of your two hour lunches someday, but I could use a little information right now."

"Hey, that is why I am here. Serving the public is what I live for, and you are the public, so tell me what this servant-of-the-people can do for you."

Aaron, pointing at the computer on Havoc's desk said, "you want to pound that thing and see if you have anything on a missing person from Woodbury, New Jersey calling himself, Jesus?"

Smiling, Havoc turned his chair toward the computer and replied, "you mean Heh-soss don't you? I think that fellow Jesus has been dead for a

79

couple of thousand years, and since we have about 35 million Hispanics in this country, I am afraid typing in Heh-soss (Jesus) will get about one million hits."

"Pronounce it any way you want, just spell it J-e-s-u-s and see if he has been reported as missing."

Enjoying the banter, Havoc said, "any last name, or do I just type in son of Mary and Joseph?"

"I have no last name, but I have a town called Woodbury Creek in South Jersey. I doubt if there are very many people there named Jesus. You going to make with the jokes or help me out?"

While Aaron was talking, John had already typed in Jesus/Missing Person/Woodbury Creek/New Jersey. Easing back in his chair and looking at Aaron, he said, "it will take a minute to search the Jersey files on CODEX. You want to tell me what this is all about?"

"Can't do that right now friend, but believe me, you will be clued in if it is as big as I think it is. You remember my old partner Dixon Long? He was burned up in a fire in Arkansas. Supposedly an accident, but it was no accident. This fellow in

80

Jersey calling himself Jesus is connected."

"Sorry to hear about Long. Never really knew him, but heard about him from you and a few of the old-timers here. Must have been a nice guy."

Aaron, somewhat pensive, replied, "the best."

Havoc perked up and looked at the computer. Reading from it and glancing at Aaron, his deep voice seemed to echo in the room. "Yeah, here you go. Man named Jesus – no last name noted, reported missing by a woman named Mary Madison one week ago in Woodbury Creek, New Jersey. Notation by local sheriff attached that says he was a known derelict who probably just left down. No known address, no close acquaintances, other than a Mary Madison and a Dixon Long. File still open but not a priority."

"Can you get me an address on Mary Madison?"

Scrolling through the file, Havoc picked up a pen and wrote down the woman's address. As he handed to Aaron, he said, "you're too old to be chasing dames. She's listed as 36 years old. I should go to Woodbury Creek with you and help you out. An old man like you just can't get the job done when it comes to a young woman."

81

Aaron, as he headed out the door, replied, "go back to serving the public, asshole."

The drive down the Garden State Parkway was just another reminder to Aaron of all that was wrong with a country he had once loved so much that he idiotically signed up to serve it during the Vietnam War. As a young man, he could have avoided service through a well-connected father, but felt if he did, then someone else would have to serve in his place. How could he sleep at night knowing that a poor ghetto youth with no political connections had died in his place. He went. He served, and he learned while being privy to top-secret information at the Pentagon, the truth about a country that wanted blind obedience from its citizens. Asking questions was tantamount to treason, because questioning authority might lead to the truth.

Looking at the mean streets of city after city, the dilapidated buildings, the homeless people meandering about pushing shopping carts, the unemployed lining the streets, the blank stares of those who had lost hope in a country that was supposed to be the envy of the world just reminded Aaron of how far he had watched the country he loved fall into the abyss of misery promulgated by a system that saw all the good things flow to those at the top.

Woodbury, like most of small-town America, had fallen into decay. Aaron had passed a Wal-Mart outside of town, which probably explained why there were so few businesses downtown. The little guy just couldn't compete with a monolithic corporation. Now, people who once owned their own businesses were working for $8.00 an hour at Wal-Mart, and the morons who ran the country called that capitalism. What a joke. Capitalism only existed in the manipulated minds of the masses who fell for all the propaganda spewed out by the wealthy and powerful who had hi-jacked a good idea and turned it into nothing more than an excuse to lock the masses into servitude.

He pulled up across from Barbara's Café, the greasy spoon where Jesus had let three people know that he would not tolerate judgemental arrogance. Aaron went directly to the nearby sheriff's office and was greeted by a woman who was busy eating a hamburger.

"Could I speak to the sheriff," said Aaron.

Putting down her burger, the woman replied, "maybe you should tell me your business before I get the sheriff."

83

Not liking her tone, Aaron replied, "I will talk to the Sheriff. He is elected by the people to serve the people. I am the people, so tell him to serve me."

Seemingly shocked at Aaron's demeanour, the woman said, "the sheriff is a busy man. You just can't walk off the street and expect to see him without an appointment or without discussing the matter with me first."

Aaron, as always, was ready to do battle with those who thought their positions of authority were a licence to make others feel beneath them. He gave her a stern look and said, "lady, I don't have time to waste. I need to talk to the sheriff."

Realizing she was fighting a losing battle, the deputy replied, "your name please."

"Aaron Adams from New York City."

Knocking on the door like a dutiful servant to her boss, a voice said, "enter."

After a few seconds she came back out and told Aaron to go in. As Aaron walked into the office, the sheriff was swivelling left to right in his chair, and did not get up.

84

Standing at the edge of the ornate oak desk, Aaron extended his hand and said, "I am Aaron Adams, a P.I. from New York City."

Before Aaron could start his next sentence, the Sheriff rose from his chair and extended his hand. Smiling he said, "I know you Adams. You've made a few headlines in your day. I remember that case about the mysterious box that damn near blew up New York City. I was just a high school kid then, but there were headlines all over the country."

Aaron, not wanting to reminisce over a case that had never really been solved and had led to a steady downhill spiral, blurted out, "I am afraid I don't have time to talk about my past cases. I am working on one now that is pretty important."

The sheriff eased back into his chair and motioned for Aaron to take a seat. It was then that the sheriff had a premonition and replied, "I bet I can guess what you are here about. Don't know why, but there seems to be a lot of interest in some nut-case who called himself Jesus and I mean J-e-s-u-s, not Heh-soos. The F.B.I., the National Security Agency and Homeland Security were all here asking about this nut-case. He caused quite a stir around here for awhile and then he just up and

85

disappeared. Seemed to have just dropped out of sight overnight. One minute he was preaching some mumbo jumbo in the park, and then, he was gone. Am I right, you here about him."

"You got it sheriff," replied Aaron, his voice rising sharply.

"I can't help you. That is all I know, except that he seemed to single me out for ridicule for serving what he called the entitled classes. Damn arrogant bastard."

Aaron, his voice seeming to deepen, said, "maybe the arrogant bastard was right. Perhaps you do represent the entitled classes. I never knew any law enforcement officers who didn't. I don't generally see them represent the poor and powerless, but they fall all over themselves when it comes to serving the interests of the privileged and connected."

Obviously growing tired of the banter, the sheriff, in a determined manner, said, "what the hell do you want Adams? I am a busy man."

Aaron, quickly glancing over his shoulder at the empty lobby, except for the deputy, replied, "yeah, I can see that you are jammed up with people who

As the Son of Thunder

are demanding service."

Continuing, Aaron calmly said, "I have it from a good authority that a Mary Madison reported this guy missing. Are you doing anything to find him?"

"Not that it is any of your business," the sheriff curtly replied, "but I know what happened to him. The same thing that happens to all vagrants who wonder through town. He headed somewhere else to create problems for another public official. These people are just looking for a handout from the folks who really work for a living. When they see they have hit up all the soft touches in a town, they just move on."

Aaron, incredulously angry with the sheriff's arrogance replied, "so, this man disappears and one of the citizens you are supposed to serve reports him missing, but you just ignore her because she has no juice."

The sheriff leaned slightly forward and pointed his right index finger directly at Aaron. "First, the guy was a trouble-maker who would have wound up in jail had he stuck around. Second, the woman who reported him missing is a known prostitute who has been in jail several times herself."

87

Aaron, warming to the verbal sparing, replied, "so, because one person is considered a trouble-maker by you, and the other person a prostitute, you think neither are worthy of consideration. Yet, if a banker, lawyer or accountant walked in here, they would get the red carpet treatment."

Aaron arose, turned, walked toward the doorway and noticed the deputy had gotten up from her seat and had her hand on her gun, seemingly ready to draw it, if Aaron caused any more disturbance.

Looking over his shoulder, his parting words left the deputy and the sheriff speechless. "You disgust me. I am going over to see Mary Madison. A prostitute at least reaches out with compassion to those who long for human warmth. You reserve all your compassion for those who need it least. The rich and well-connected are your masters, but they aren't mine. I will find this guy Jesus, and I just hope you are some way implicated in his disappearance, because there is nothing I like better than bringing down arrogant people like you. I am here to make sure Mary Madison isn't ignored. You are dealing with Aaron Adams. I am dynamite and sometimes I explode."

Aaron exited the sheriff's office building, turned to his right and headed briskly toward his car. His

As the Son of Thunder

stride quickened as he noticed a man in a dark suit seemingly bending over the back of his car. A horn honked and the man suddenly stood erect, turned and walked down the street and got into a black sedan driven by another man in a dark suit.

Aaron intentionally ignored the men in the car, being careful not to turn his head their way. He got in, buckled up, pulled away from the curb and headed for Mary Madison's apartment.

Before leaving New York City, he had used his computer to get the directions to her place. Picking up the printed directions and glancing down at them, he knew all he had to do was turn around and go back down Main Street to her apartment building. Looking in his rear view mirror, he noticed the black sedan was a few hundred feet behind him. Turning on the first street to his right, the sedan continued down the Main Street. Aaron pulled into a parking lot, backed-up and went back toward Main Street. Turning left, he headed toward Mary Madison's. Instinctively, he glanced in his rear view mirror, and there it was – the black sedan was behind him again. The sedan continued to follow him to Mary Madison's apartment building. As he pulled to the curb, the sedan continued up the street and turned right into another apartment building parking lot.

89

Getting out of his car, Aaron glanced up the street and saw the black sedan pull into the street and park on the right side. It didn't take a genius to figure out they were government men. Just which branch of the government? They were so many jack-booted government Nazis roaming the country since 9/11 that it was hard to take a piss without someone knowing the size of your dick. Americans were too stupid to realize that their government was nothing more than a corporate/religious theocracy that spied on them day and night to keep them in line, so the so-called democracy the citizens had been propagandized into believing they had could be protected from the media manufactured evil-doers. The real evil doer was the U.S. government and their corporate and religious masters.

The apartment building was old and dilapidated. It was just another monument to greed that kept a permanent underclass of citizens to serve the needs of the well-off. Aaron remembered what he had once read in a book. "Without a working class, there would be no privileged class."

It was a four story building made of grey stone. It had been built at the turn of the century, a time when there were still artisans who took pride in their craft. Even the disrepair of the building could

90

not mask the beauty and grace of an era when people who worked with their hands were prized. Now, the barons of excess in banks and on Wall Street were the pride of a society where greed was proclaimed a virtue. What was built today was nothing but homogenized, boring, cheap monuments to a throw-away society that had no place for those who created with their hands rather than with their calculators and computers.

There was a thin blond woman, maybe 17 or 18 years old, sitting on the entrance steps smoking a cigarette. She was holding a child of about two years old, blowing smoke in its face. You had to get a licence to drive, but there was no licence required to have children. Just another child the Christians insisted be born who would be swallowed up by poverty. The same Christians would insist that it was the mother's responsibility to provide medical insurance for the child in a nation where healthcare was a privilege rather than a right. Then those same Christians would demand an eye for eye as punishment when the child broke the law in order to survive in a nation where the rich preyed upon the poor. What a world.

As Aaron walked past the woman, she looked up at him with eyes that seemed to symbolize a deep

91

longing for justice from a society where there was none. Aaron smiled to let her know he cared, but there was nothing he could do, because he was just another one of the powerless cogs in the machine of misery that ground up people like sausage in a meat grinder.

As he walked into the atrium, he looked to his right and saw the list of tenants and their apartment numbers on the wall. The third one down read apartment 1-C, Mary Madison. Looking to his right, he could see the apartment about 30 feet down the walkway. As he strolled briskly toward the apartment, he noticed the back of a woman in the atrium who was on her knees playing with several children and a small cat. An old woman, probably in her 80's, stood over the woman smiling broadly at her antics with the cat and children. Aaron rang the bell on 1-C. He was still slightly turned toward the atrium, fascinated by the back of the woman who was still playing with the children and cat. He thought to himself how lovely this woman must be, because her back was partly bare, as the blouse she had on went under her arm on the right side, exposing a beautiful shoulder.

The old lady sighted Aaron ringing the bell and bent over to whisper something to the woman.

92

As Aaron rang the bell again, the squatting woman got to her feet. From about 30 feet away, Aaron could see the lady slowly turn and begin to move toward him. Her long, smooth strides seemed like slow motion from a movie. Her ample breasts bounced provocatively as she smoothly strode across the grass toward Aaron. The silken dress that was about an inch above the knees seemed to hug her every curve, accentuating her womanliness in every possible way. The 60 year old Aaron, for the first time in years, felt a tingle between his legs. Nearing within a few feet of him, a smile slowly creased across her lips, showing pearly, white, even teeth, as she said "are you looking for me, sir?" Aaron was frozen in place as he stood in silence.

Aaron looked into her eyes and he was resurrected. He had been dead so long, but it was as if the hand of God had reached down and touched him. He had been looking for someone for what seemed like an eternity. He knew her name in the countless fantasies that preyed on his mind. He knew where she lived in his sojourns of nightly slumber that brought him peace, but this was the first time that he had seen her in the flesh. He remembered the Bible from the years he had been brainwashed as a child by his relatives, and the Sunday school teachers who used fear and

93

intimidation to force rote memory of a book that was filled with violence and evil. How many times had he heard that charm was deceitful and beauty was vain. Yet, this woman's beauty showed no vanity, and the charm was genuine as she smiled appealingly with a warmth that seemed to come from the heart. The outward beauty was overwhelming, but the true beauty of this woman was in her soul. She was filled with love. You could tell it because the children, the old woman and even the cat turned to watch as she walked away. They were all drawn to her periphery of love like moths to a flame. It did not boast. It was not self-seeking. It kept no records of wrongs or slights. It simply persevered. It reached out with compassion, hope and understanding. Aaron was in heaven and the gates had been swung open by an angel.

Stumbling for words, Aaron mumbled, "are you Mary Madison?"

As she replied, "yes, I am she," the sun peaked over the top floor of the apartment building, bathing the atrium in bright light and the streaming rays flickered about her long, thick, dark hair seemingly forming a halo effect above her head. Still mesmerized, all Aaron could muster was, "I, I, I'm................"

As the Son of Thunder

Smiling more broadly, Mary said, "are you alright? Come inside and I will get you a cold drink of water."

Shaking his head as if coming out of a deep slumber, Aaron recovered his senses and replied, "Yes, that would be nice. I am Aaron Adams, and I need to speak with you about a man calling himself Jesus and a friend of mine named Dixon Long."

As Mary opened her door to usher Aaron in, she replied, "Yes, Dixon said that he would be contacting you. I heard of his accident just yesterday. He was such a nice man, and in the brief time I knew him, I genuinely felt we had become friends."

Mary pointed at a large, overstuffed chair indicating that Aaron should have a seat. As she moved gracefully toward the adjoining kitchen, Aaron eased into the chair, watching every willowy glide of her hips that swayed provocatively from side to side, the fabric of her dress clinging seductively to her body. There was that tingle again between Aaron's legs. He struggled for words and managed to mumble, "Dixon Long's death was no accident, and your friend's disappearance is highly suspicious, too."

95

Returning from the kitchen with a glass of water, as Mary handed it to Aaron with her dainty, soft hands she said, "no accident? What do you mean?"

"Dixon was killed by the F.B.I., and it had something to do with the disappearance of your friend who was calling himself Jesus."

Mary, consternation creeping across her face, backed toward the sofa across from Aaron and sit down. Looking perplexed she said, "you are telling me that the government killed Dixon?"

Aaron, knowing that he could trust this woman with the darkest of secrets, replied, "I am."

"How do you know that?"

Aaron without hesitating replied, "I was there. Two F.B.I. agents came into Dixon's house with guns blazing. I managed to kill them, but they got Dixon first. He died in my arms, pleading for me to come to Woodbury. The F.B.I. burned his house to cover up what happened. Supposedly, Dixon caused the fire by falling asleep with a cigarette in his hand. Typical of the government, they never let the truth get in the way of their salacious lies. Dixon didn't smoke."

96

Still overcome with emotion, Mary reached up to her thick, sultry, red lips and gently rubbed them with her thumb and index finger. She was trancelike, as she said, "Dixon murdered and Jesus disappearing. They must be related. But why would the government - why would anybody want to do these things to them? They were both gentle souls who only reached out with love to lift up those who bore the burdens of cruelty in a world that is sorely lacking in compassion. Why? Why?"

Aaron eased forward in the chair and said, "I don't know why, but I can assure you that I intend to find out why. Dixon was my friend, and nobody, the government included, will get away with the murder of my friend. Most Americans sit idly by as their government tortures, murders and locks up those who question the tyranny of evil perpetrated by the thugs who call themselves our protectors. I don't fear death, because I have been dead for so long, anyway. I will find out what happened to your friend, because it is connected to Dixon's death. The government has awakened Aaron Adams, and I am an avenging angel."

Mary crossed her legs, exposing her provocative, soft, silky thighs. There was that tingle again between an old man's legs.

As the Son of Thunder

CHAPTER 9
THIS GUY IS A TERRORIST

As difficult as it was, Aaron knew that he had to get his mind off the sexual arousal that he felt being in the presence of such a provocative woman. Anyway, he was too old for this type of youthful infatuation. What interest would a young woman, obviously highly desirable to all men, have in an old, beaten-down shell of a man who was 60 and looked it? His wrinkled face, the eyes that carried heavy baggage, the slightly crooked nose that had been bent from being broken too many times, and the scar on his cheek from the time he almost lost a battle with a switch blade, all made him less than the pretty boy most women expected in a country where the plastic world of Madison Avenue defined what constituted an appealing man or woman.

Mary, smiling slightly through those gorgeous, full, ripe lips, uncrossed her legs, and in doing so, exposed that provocative area on the inside of her thighs for a slight second. Aaron knew he had to get hold of his passion. He was too old for this kind of nonsense. Yet, the rise he felt in his pants made him feel alive for the first time in years. This woman had brought back a passion to his life that he thought was long gone.

98

Aaron, breaking the tense silence, said, "I need to know all you can tell me about this man calling himself Jesus. Dixon provided me with a little information, but I want to know anything that might help me locate him. That means I need information about what went on here in Woodbury Creek. Tell me what happened, when it happened and where it happened. I am an atheist and refuse to believe in the nonsense promulgated by those who want to manipulate all humanity, but I am willing to accept all possibilities in reviewing this situation. Jesus, in my opinion, is nothing but a fairy tale produced by a pack of self-serving hypocrites. I got over fairy tales when I was about 7 years old. However, Dixon Long was my friend, and he believed in the sanctity of this man. I think he was killed as a result of his association with him. Somebody will pay for Dixon's death, two already have, but there are others and they will also pay. I will see to that."

Mary, looking with a sense of amazement at Aaron, replied, "I shall share all I can, but first you need to know his appearance, because that alone set him apart from any man I have ever known. You, Aaron, are unique in looks and demeanour. I can see the rough exterior of a man who is afraid of nothing, a man who has endured great tribulations, a person who has seen the worst

99

of the human spirit. Yet, I see a kind, caring heart beneath that rough exterior and veneer of invincibility. I say these things to you, because I want you to know that I am a perceptive judge of character. You know your true-self, but hide it beneath a mask of toughness that only a few can see beyond."

Aaron could say nothing in response. He simply sit in silence as this remarkable woman seemed to penetrate his very soul and lay his inner most being bare. Mary continued, "this man called Jesus was the most perfect human being I have ever seen. His face was noble and lively, with fair and slightly wavy chestnut hair that fell to his shoulders, thick and strongly curving eyebrows, intense penetrating dark eyes that exhibited an expression of wondrous grace and peace. His nose was long and noble. His moderately thick chestnut beard seemed to add a touch of wisdom to his demeanour. Although he strode about with confidence, it was a quiet confidence that showed no arrogance. Oh, but what an aura of gravity and wisdom seemed to permeate from the words that flowed melodically from his mouth. When attacking hypocrisy, his courteous and fair manner never faltered, but you could sense the emotion that came from deep within as he admonished those who only cared for themselves."

100

Aaron leaned back in his chair, mesmerized by the convictive way Mary seemed to revere this man who had, no doubt, been only a small part of her life for a brief period of time. Aaron was amazed how a man who obviously rebuked majesty, counselled with mildness, eloquence and gravity could make such a profound impression on two people like Dixon Long and Mary Madison. In spite of having never met the man, Aaron, himself, was already somewhat in awe of him.

What follows is the tale of Jesus as imparted emotionally to Aaron by Mary Madison. Like the New Testament's books of Matthew, Mark, Luke and John, there would, no doubt, be some discrepancies based upon various witnesses to the events. Yet, great credence can be placed on the account provided by Mary, who was constantly by the side of this man calling himself Jesus. Aaron saw Christianity and the accounts of Jesus as nothing more than fairy tales promulgated by a society that used religion as just one of many methods to keep its citizens in bondage. Yet, he could not discount the veracity of Mary Madison, even though she was a woman society frowned upon, because she made her living by providing sexual favours to men. A corrupt, hypocritical society had disdain for her, but Aaron saw her as a tower of virtue in a sea of sanctimonious deceit.

101

What follows is translated from the first person as told by Mary to Aaron that night as he sit mesmerized listening to her summarization of the few days she and Dixon spent with this extraordinary man.

Mary's Tales of Jesus and his Teachings

Jesus became fast friends with Dixon and Mary. In these two people he saw modern day disciples. They were both on the fringes of a society that demanded conventionality from all its citizens. Yet, Jesus felt that these two could understand that he was not just the prince of peace, but also an extremist for the cause of justice.

On that day in the park these two disciples had overheard a minister in the crowd of on-lookers utter the words, "he is dangerous." Both immediately knew that their friend was in trouble, because those who stood in the pulpits of America's churches wielded inordinate power in a country that professed freedom of religion, but refused to accept anyone who questioned the authority of religion. It was a country where freedom of religion did not mean freedom from religion. And this man was preaching against organized religion and its propensity for self-indulgence.

These religious paragons of virtue were the real extremists who depended on trickery, lies, coercion, fear and terrorism to force people to bow before repression. They were committed to the status-quo that kept them in power.

As the ministers banded together and walked away, Jesus pointed at them and said, "I have disdain for all that modern religion stands for in a society that does not know the meaning of true compassion. Bring a voice of hope to the people and you are labelled a radical. Well, I am a radical and proud of it. Ask yourself when you attend church on Sundays if these men of God fight for progressive social change? Do they further the interests of ordinary working people or of the powerful and wealthy? Do they encourage workers to fight for social change and justice in the workplace? As they turn their backs and walk away from the truth, these are just a few of the questions you should ask them."

Smiling as the ministers continued walking from the park, Jesus waved his right hand over the throng of people and continued his admonitions. "As these supposed purveyors of God's word walk away from the light, be eternally vigilant in seeking the truth by questioning authority. Do not teach your children to meekly accept what they are

103

taught in schools run by the church or state that preach blind obedience to authority. Teach your children to be extremists by demanding an answer for why there is homelessness in a land of plenty. Have them demand an answer for why healthcare is only for those who can afford it. Demand that they question why everyone cannot be guaranteed a job. Teach them to embrace defiance to unjustness in any form. That is why I have been slaughtered many times. Yet, I still stand before you. I am still trying to give you the courage to stand with me against those who enslave you."

The crowd broke out in spontaneous applause, and there were shouts of "yeah, yeah, tell it like it is."

Mary and Dixon looked on in disbelief at the power of his words. Jesus continued. "We all are faced with two roads. There is the modern road paved with stones of gold that lures us into thinking that material possessions are the path to happiness. This road has damaged and seared the earth, but more crudely, it has damaged your souls. This is the road to destruction. Then, there is the alternative road of compassion and love. It is a slower path that has been travelled by too few people. The trail is not paved, but rather is green with grass and is pure. It recognizes the power and

104

and majesty of the earth that is plentiful with the bounty that must be shared by all in equal proportions, with no man having too little nor no man having too much. This is the road all those with love and compassion for their fellow man must follow."

Looking at several Native Americans who were standing in the crowd, Jesus pointed directly at them and said, "your ancestors knew that you do not sell the earth upon which people walk. The people's birthright is not for sale. The land is more valuable than money. It will last forever. It cannot perish in flame. As long as the sun shines and the water flows, all men can share it. It belongs to everyone, and it is time you reclaimed it and shared it with all humanity rather than allowing the greedy to fence it off and defile it in the name of progress."

A well-dressed businessman in the back of the crowd shouted to Jesus, "but can you not see that we have a right to resent those who do not contribute to society?"

Jesus then began a parable. "Two men were seriously ill in a hospital room. One had to spend his time on his back and could not move. He frequently asked the other man, whom he assumed

105

was next to a window, to describe to him what was going on outside. For weeks the man enlivened the other patient's spirits by describing the beautiful park outside the window, the hues of the sky, the lovely pond nearby filled with ducks and swans, the children sailing their boats, the grand trees and the frequent rainbows. He even described a parade that went by."

Jesus paused for a few seconds, looked down at the spiral notebook that he always carried, flipped the page and continued, "soon the immoveable patient began to resent the man by the window. Why should that man have the pleasure of seeing all the beauty of the outside world? It didn't seem fair. His envy grew into resentment and it turned him sour. He was abrupt and rude with the man by the window. Eventually, he would not speak to him at all, deciding that silence was better than hearing a description of beauty he could only imagine and not see."

"Late one night as this man lay looking up at the ceiling, the individual by the window starting coughing and gagging for breath. He died that night, and the other man could hardly wait to ask the nurse to move him next to the window. The next day, when the nurse moved him, he could not wait to look out at all the beauty. Disappointment immediately set in when he realized that there was no lake outside, no ducks, no swans, no children sailing boats and no trees. You could barely even see the sky, as within a few feet of the window was the back of a row of steel two story buildings that obscured the view."

"Lowering his head, the man asked the nurse if the man was crazy, because he had described such a beautiful view. The nurse simply replied that the man could see nothing, because he was blind."

Then, looking directly at the man who asked the question, Jesus continued, "my friend, those of us with eyes are often blind. Yet, those without sight can sometimes see things that never were, and dream things that should be. There are those who might say the blind man was a burden on society. Do not point the finger of condemnation at those you think do not contribute, because no matter how innocuous the gift from those on the margins of a society where a person's worth is judged by the size of his bank account, all deeds of kindness, no matter how small, are recorded in the book of life."

The man who asked the question hung his head and faded into the crowd. Meanwhile, Jesus was on a roll and continued his spell-binding rhetoric.

107

Looking out at the crowd that had now grown to maybe 500, Jesus pointed toward the sky and said, "do not look up there for heaven. Look into your heart and the hearts of others. The heart can be a lonely hunter. Do not depend on a big black book for guidance. The Bible you read is filled with contradictions, but there are no contradictions in the depths of one's heart, which is the mirror of the soul. The parable I just shared is illustrative of how we must look beyond what we see with our eyes. We must also see with the heart."

The crowd, growing ever larger as word spread about this wise sage who was holding court in the park, was silent as Jesus' voice echoed with a grace that none there had ever experienced before. Each tree, each plant, each blade of grass seemed bathed in serenity.

This was Jesus' moment and he knew it. In a calm tone, he invoked all in the back not to push, because his voice, no matter how soft, could always be heard if they would just listen. It was then that he shared the parable of the college graduate who rebuked his father for what he thought was a slight. "There was a young man from a struggling family whose father worked hard to send to college. The son had always been spoiled and was provided with many amenities, as

108

the father wanted him to have the things he, himself, had been denied as a child. Upon graduation, the son expected that the father would provide him with a lavish gift like most of his contemporaries were getting. Instead, the father gave him a leather bound album of pictures he had accumulated over the years the two of them shared together. He told the son, within this album you will find the keys of my love."

"The son simply said thanks, took the album and sauntered off to his room, threw it in a drawer and never saw it again. Getting a job in a distant city, he became successful, reared a wonderful family and generally ignored his dad. When he was 50 years old, he got word that his father had died at the age of 82 in an old-age facility. Having not seen his dad in years, he did not attend the funeral, and he was told over the phone by the executor of his dad's estate that his entire inheritance would be mailed to him in a small box, as most of the estate had been depleted by the time of his death."

"The son saw no need to return home and watch a casket be lowered into a grave. Receiving the material left behind by his father, the son went through it piece by piece, throwing everything into the trash, as there was not only nothing of monetary value, but the son felt there was also nothing of sentimental value, as he had long ago decided his father was not important in his life."

Jesus reached up to his brow and wiped away a bead of sweat. He continued. "The son was down to the last item in the box, the album his father had given him for graduation many years before. For some reason, he flipped through it in an unsentimental fashion, ignoring most of the photos. Then on the last page, tucked in the plastic cover was an envelope. The man removed it and gently tore it open. A key fell onto the table. He picked it up and examined it closely, but could not figure out why it was there. In the envelope was a small piece of paper. The man removed it and was shocked at what it said."

"Dear son, I have been making payments on a house since you were 2 years old. Two days before your graduation, I paid off the mortgage. This is the key to your new home, and I hope you will give me the privilege of spending time with you there on occasion, because I value the time I spend with you so much. Love, your adoring father."

The crowd stood in contemplative silence and Jesus said, "so I plead with you to not accept everything at face value. Look beyond your initial impression and search for the truth. Be like the aforementioned blind man, see things as they should be, not as they are."

"I implore each one of you here today to heed my words and reflect on my parables. Then, stop being complacent and demand fairness from those who keep you in invisible chains. If you feel you are not in bondage, look at you fellow man, and if you see him in bondage, then realize that if there is but one human in chains, it is incumbent upon you to remove them together."

Jesus saw three men in dark suits mingling in the crowd, seeming to push people out of their way as they moved toward the front. Realizing that the sun was starting to go down, Jesus said, "I conclude for now, but will be here again at noon tomorrow, provided I am not incarcerated by those who fear me. As you go home tonight, think about what I have said today, and remember that a nation run by fake Christians, fake politicians, fake protectors and fake prophets is not worthy of respect. You are the enablers of these people who turn on you and put you in chains. Look at your condition and then look at the palatial mansions where your oppressors live. I am here to lead a revolution, but revolution is not without consequences for those of us who refuse to bend

111

before the winds of tyranny. I have been condemned before and I will be condemned again by those who fear the truth. There are those among you now who plot my demise."

The crowd was stunned by his announcement, and as they dispersed, they looked all about them, as if they were trying to identify those who would betray this wise man. Unfortunately, they were unaware that most in the crowd would betray him, not because they did not believe in his message, but because they feared those in authority more than they loved the freedom offered by this sage's words.

As Jesus got down from the picnic table, Mary and Dixon were waiting for him. Also waiting were the three men in dark suits, who immediately came up to Jesus. All three methodically removed their ID badges from their coat pockets and flashed them in unison, as if they had practiced the procedure for maximum effect.

Jesus, without hesitation, said, "am I supposed to be impressed with those symbols of authority? Do you think I fear those who serve the oppressors. I represent people with no voice or power. I am an anarchist. And remember that anarchy in the name of justice is purity."

112

Taken aback by his boldness, the men stood in silence for a second as Dixon said, "do you have any reason to detain this man?"

One of them replied, "we are the F.B.I. and under the Patriot Act, we don't need a reason to detain anyone we suspect of either fomenting, encouraging or engaging in what might be termed terrorism."

Mary Madison, emboldened by the presence of Jesus and what he had taught, said, "gentlemen this man has done nothing wrong. He has taught us all to stop being afraid to face those who enslave us. The real terrorists are men like you in suits, in corporate boardrooms and in the highest echelons of government."

Jesus, smiling at the audaciousness of his most recent convert, said, "do not chastise them too much, because they, like so many others, have been brainwashed into believing they are the righteous purveyors of justice in a land of mass injustice. Gentlemen, I shall listen to what you have to say, but I refuse to bow in supplication before you or any other man. Ask your questions and I will answer truthfully, but do not expect me to cower in fear before you just because you have badges."

113

A man with white hair, apparently the senior agent, said, "we have received information that you are encouraging people to commit acts of violence."

Jesus responded calmly, "how do you get the attention of those who will not listen? Was it the civil rights marchers who got the attention of legislators through peaceful demonstrations or was it those who started burning down America's cities who finally got the attention of the power structure? The F.B.I. committed acts of violence against the Black Panthers, against the American Indian Movement, against the anti-war movement and against the civil rights movement. Yet, it was called justice by your side. The government commits acts of violence when it refuses to provide healthcare to a dying child whose parents are penniless. The Congress commits acts of violence when it allows the rich to get a free ride on the backs of the middle class and poor. Do not talk to me about violence while you condone the violence of the oppressors. Remember that one man's terrorist is another man's freedom fighter."

The white haired man was surprised by the directness of Jesus and said, "I am not here to investigate past wrongs. I am here to prevent any future wrongs."

114

Jesus placed his right hand on the man's coat sleeve and replied, "there would be no future wrongs but for the wrongs of the past."

The youngest of the three agents, seemingly in his 20's, said in an arrogant manner, "listen asshole, we represent the full authority of the U.S. government, and we don't need any lecture from a scraggily haired bum who thinks he is the messiah."

Jesus, warming to the verbal sparring, said, "but I am the messiah. I am the man who lays the truth bare before all, so they can decide for themselves whether they want to continue in slavery or throw off the chains that keep them in bondage. You, too, are in bondage, but you cannot see your chains. You are blinded by patriotic babble and a belief in your innate superiority. Make no mistake, in my eyes, you are not exalted among men. The exalted ones are those who toil in the fields of despair for minimal monetary returns so that men like you can walk around in $500 suits feeling superior."

The white haired man interrupted and said, "enough of this bull-shit banter. We are here to simply tell you that we have our eyes on you, and that if you go too far, your ass will be locked up."

As the Son of Thunder

As Jesus turned to walk away with Mary and Dixon, he looked over his shoulder and left the three men with profound partying words that would plague them. "You can physically lock me up, but you can never imprison my mind. You can kill me, but you can never kill my ideas."

That evening Dixon, Mary and Jesus all had dinner at the diner. While sharing the meal, Jesus said to Dixon and Mary, "I am proud of the courage you both showed today. Yet, I must alert you that being my friend has gotten many individuals into a great deal of trouble over the years. In fact, many have lost their lives in defence of me."

Dixon replied, "I am not afraid. I have lived in fear for too many years."

Mary smiled and said, "nor am I fearful. You have showed me that living in fear is not living at all."

"You two have learned that you can crowd a life-time into an hour. It is better to die free than to live a slave. I just hope some of the others whom I have touched here will feel as you do. I cannot promise anyone eternal life, but I can promise them a more abundant life."

116

As the three got up to leave, in the booth beside them, a father was chastising and berating his young son for striking out with the bases loaded at a Little League baseball game. Jesus stopped and politely said, "sir, may I offer a bit of advice?"

The man, rather burly in size, replied, "what the hell advice do you have for me?"

Turning to Dixon, Jesus said, "give me a $20 bill, Dixon."

Dixon dutifully reached into his wallet and handed Jesus a $20 bill. Jesus said, "would you like this $20?"

"I ain't no fool. Sure, if you are stupid enough to give away $20, I will take it."

As the people at other tables began to listen to what was going on, Jesus smiled and crumbled up the $20 bill. Then he asked the man if he still wanted it even though it was crumbled up? The man replied, "yes, it is still a $20 bill."

Then Jesus threw the bill to the floor, stepped on it and ground it with his feet. Picking the bill up, he then calmly asked the man, "do you still want it?"

117

"Of course, it is still a $20 bill."

Jesus flipped the bill on the table in front of the man and said, "no matter what I did to the $20 bill, it was still valuable. You still wanted it. Think about that and ask yourself if your son's mistake at bat made him any less valuable to you? Is he not still the same boy he was before he struck out?"

The man lowered his head slightly but turned his eyes up toward his son, as if pleading for forgiveness. Jesus turned, signalled for Dixon and Mary to follow him out of the now totally quiet diner.

On the way back to Mary's apartment, the three strolled nonchalantly through downtown Woodbury Creek. Suddenly, Mary's right hand brushed against the left hand of Jesus. She instinctively gripped his hand. Not letting go, Jesus looked straight ahead and began a story.

"There was a woman who had trouble discerning the difference between love and friendship. When she told her father she was in love, he simply asked her if her heart beat faster when she was in the man's presence. When she replied that she was much more apt to smile than have a racing heart,

118

her father told her that it was friendship, not love."

Jesus, looking slightly to his left at Mary, continued, "you must know the difference."

Mary, realizing that she was indeed nothing more than a friend with this man, let go of his hand. Jesus reached down, grasp her hand and said, "there is nothing wrong with friends holding hands." At the same time, he reached over and took Dixon's hand. The three of them strolled down the street, as others looked on quizzically. Yet, they had no shame.

As they arrived in front of Mary's apartment, Dixon noticed a black sedan moving slowly behind them. When it passed, he observed the silvery white hair of the driver, and realized it was the three F.B.I. agents. They pulled to the curb a few feet beyond the apartment. Jesus smiled at Dixon and said, "do not worry about the F.B.I., as I have had much more intrepid, evil pursuers in the past. Let us go in and share an evening snack, so we can discuss today's events and what might ensue tomorrow."

While they enjoyed a snack prepared by all three of them, Jesus noticed that Dixon Long seemed especially pensive. He looked at Mary pensively

119

and said, "our friend Dixon keeps glancing out the window, looking for those three men whom he fears will harm me. Mary, you and he must not fear for me. I have suffered greatly at the hands of many over the years. Though physically painful, that part of the pain is endurable. The true pain comes from knowing that your fellow sojourners in life have so little personal strength that they are willing to do the bidding of those who enslave them. Those who torture also torture themselves, but they are too brainwashed to realize it."

Dixon, concerned about his new found friend said, "why don't you get out of this place, get out of this country. Go somewhere that is not in the constant grip of fear as this nation is. There are countries where freedom really does exist and is not just a figment of a brainwashed public's imagination."

Jesus, in his customarily quiet, direct demeanour replied, "I have learned that those who are most religious are most fearful. Religion is a by-product of fear. This nation is the most fearful on earth. Yet, rather than fear other countries, the citizens should fear their own country, because this is a nation infested with those who maximize their control through religious babble and senseless patriotic absurdities. That is why I need to arouse

120

the people here. They must be awakened from their slumber. The people of this nation are locked in the evil grip of religious servitude to an idea of the son-of-man that is entirely false. Those who preach about God base their manifestations on fear of the vilest form – fear of the mysterious, fear of defeat, fear of death and fear of a vengeful deity. They make religion a disease born of fear that has brought untold misery to the citizens of this country and the rest of the world. Until people free themselves of this malignancy, there will never be any peace."

Dixon, as always perplexed by this man's approach to religion, said, "but you seem to have disdain for religion, when you are supposed to be promoting it."

"My friend, I have disdain for anyone who lets their faith get in the way of the truth. For too many believers, they simply blind themselves to facts that are easily evident. The Bible is not my book, nor is Christianity my religion. I would never subject anyone to the evil perpetrated by Christian dogma. The Bible is like all other religious books, filled with fables and myths that any inquiring mind would immediately question and discard. The God I know does not reward and punish the objects of his creation."

121

Again, mystified and overwhelmed with the wisdom of this man who seemed to never accept the sanctity of the Bible or Christianity, Dixon simply smiled. Silently, he wondered how this man could survive in a country where those who questioned authority were locked-up or hounded into obscurity.

Jesus, seeing Dixon was in deep thought about what he had said, got up and walked toward the kitchen. He looked over his right shoulder and said, "Remember that those who believe in absurdities will easily commit atrocities. The illumination of the mind is stymied by religion and a government that fears an inquiring and intelligent populace."

The rest of the evening passed peacefully and the next morning Dixon and Mary got up, shared breakfast with Jesus and prepared for another day basking in the glorious manifestations promulgated by the most knowledgeable man they had ever known. It would be a day they would both never forget.

Strolling through downtown Woodbury Creek, they encountered Sheriff Dillon as he was getting out of his car. The Sheriff sarcastically said to Jesus, "planning another day of rebel-rousing?"

Jesus, in his calm demeanour replied, "this country was founded by rebel-rousers who defied authority. They would be ashamed of what this nation has become, and you should be ashamed of enforcing the unjust laws promulgated by the ruling classes whom you serve."

The sheriff, again bested by this unassuming man, shook his head and walked into his office. Meanwhile, Jesus and his two adoring friends continued down the street. As they got to the corner, Dixon noticed a black sedan driven by a white haired man was moving slowly up the street about 100 feet behind them. Jesus, putting his hand on Dixon's left arm said, "do not fret my friend. The three F.B.I. agents following us are just a few of the many who will work toward my demise. It is just part of the pattern borne out of fear – fear of the truth, fear of change and fear of inquiring minds that might question authority. They are weak vassals in service to those who manipulate and use them to maintain control."

"But why do you not fear those who seek to destroy you?"

Jesus looked forlornly at Dixon. "Fear is what keeps the people of this nation in bondage. Eliminate your fear and you destroy their power."

123

Mary said, "but how can you stand-up to them? They represent the government, and they are ruthless if you do not submit. I want to be brave. I want to demand fairness and justice, but I am fearful of death."

Jesus looked at Mary and said, "he who fears death too much will never know the true meaning of living. It is not how long one lives that counts. It is the way one lives. Remember when I told you that it is possible to crowd a lifetime into an hour? Think about the moments in your life when you felt really alive. They are few, but they were so intense they stayed with you a life-time. When fighting for justice and the innate dignity of mankind, every minute is like that."

Suddenly, the three realized that their discussion had drawn several on-lookers who seemed to be hanging on very word of wisdom Jesus shared. He continued. "So, we need not be afraid. We can all lay claim to the possibilities that are within our grasp, if we are only willing to make the sacrifice. Injustice should not be tolerated, even when it hides behind a mask of legitimacy sanctioned by a government that serves only the privileged. In a society that values those most who produce the least, dignity is corroded by poverty. When one man is poor, we are all poor."

124

Realizing they had strolled to the park and that there were now at least 50 people around him, Jesus mounted the picnic table again, waved his right hand across the crowd and continued speaking as the crowd grew steadily larger. "Today, this nation is hostile to anyone who stands against poverty. It has made poverty a disease that it refuses to cure with a fair redistribution of income from the top to the bottom. Rather, it insists all the burdens of society be placed on those in the middle or at the bottom. This unjustness must be challenged. My father in heaven is appalled by those who, in his name, sanctify greed as an enviable trait."

"A true servant of my father, the Reverend Tommy Douglas of Saskatchewan, many years ago told the story of Mouseland. It seems that little mice lived and played in a pretty nice place, much as you do here. They had an election every 4 years where they elected a government made up of fat black cats. Strange that mice would elect big cats to run their government, but it seems that was the only ones running for office. For some reason, the mice never thought they should run one of their own for office. Seems they felt they weren't fat enough to do the job. Now, I am not saying anything against big black cats. Some of them were pretty nice, but they kept passing laws that

125

were not very good for mice. One law said that a mouse hole had to be big enough for a cat's paw to fit in it. Another law required mice to walk rather than run, because that way cats could get their meals without too much effort."

The crowd, as typical of Americans, who only have U.S. heroes, was unaware of who Tommy Douglas was, and how he made universal free healthcare a guaranteed right in Canada. Yet, as the crowd grew ever larger, now numbering at least 300, they seemed to hang on every word.

"All the laws were good laws. Well, good laws for cats that is. However, life seemed to get harder and harder for the mice, but they kept electing big black cats to office, because they really had no choice. Then, they decided they could exercise some power, so they went to the polls and elected big, fat white cats to office, because the white cats had run a brilliant campaign offering to change big round mouse holes to big square mouse holes. Unfortunately, the square holes now made it possible for the cats to get both their paws into the holes. This made things tougher than ever for the mice. So, they voted white cats out and put the big black back cats in again. Nothing changed, so they put the white cats back in. Still, nothing changed, so they

126

put some white cats and some black cats in. Then, they even put in some spotted cats that instead of meowing, made noises that sounded like mice. Still, they were all cats and seemed to never pass any laws that were helpful to mice."

"The trouble wasn't the colour of the cats, the size of the cats or the noise the cats made. The trouble was that they were all cats. Therefore, they only looked after the welfare of cats."

"Finally, a little mouse came along with an idea. He said why don't we elect a government made up of mice and look out for ourselves for a change? Needless to say, the cats called him a communist and locked him up in jail."

"That is what will always happen to those who fight injustice, but always remember: you can lock up a mouse or a man, but you can never lock up an idea. If enough people stand against injustice, there will not be enough jails to incarcerate all of us."

As the crowd applauded wildly, the three F.B.I. agents were moving methodically toward Jesus. He looked down at them and said, "the big fat cats are among us. Do not fear them. It is they who should fear us?

Suddenly frightened, the white haired one motioned for them all to leave. Placing their hands at the ready to draw their guns, they quickly moved up to and then behind the picnic table and quickly exited the park.

Jesus, holding his right hand up to quiet the crowd, said, "be aware that those who seek my demise shall never waver in the pursuit of me. Those men retreat, but they will return. My message is treasonous to a nation that wants to keep you in chains. I am here to free you, if you will only listen. Many have listened in the past, but few continue to serve the cause of justice once I am gone. Remember me, and remember my call for you to disregard what those in the pulpits of hypocrisy have told you."

"My message has been twisted and warped to suit those who enslave you. First and foremost, I am a radical. I abhor injustice, and I demand that those who serve God tear down the walls that are erected to imprison people in ignorance. I refuse to support the status-quo and demand that those less fortunate among us be accorded the dignity all of us deserve. There is always a fight going on between good and evil. You can tell the evil ones easily. They are those who point the finger of condemnation and tell those on the margins of this

128

greed based economic system that they are not worthy of the good life. They use fear and intimidation to keep you in bondage."

A man in the crowd shouted to Jesus, "but we have much to fear from other countries that envy our way of life. They want to destroy us."

Jesus said to him, "name any nation that has more bombs and bullets than this one. Name any nation this rich that does not have a more equitable distribution of the bounty. You are not envied. You are feared. If you rule with bombs and bullets, why would you be surprised when you get bombs and bullets back? Which is a greater terrorist, one who flies planes into buildings, or one who lobs missiles from thousands of miles away? It takes a certain amount of courage to sacrifice your life by flying a plane into a building. How much courage does it take to push a button that will send a missile to decimate innocent women and children for the sake of revenge?"

As always with Jesus' responses, this questioner was humbled with an answer that cut to the heart of the matter. Thinking about what was said, the man nodded his head in agreement, as if to say that he had never thought of it that way, and most of the crowd was awed by what they heard.

129

An elderly woman shouted, "but the Bible says an eye for an eye and a tooth for a tooth."

"That is the Old Testament that is filled with myths. Do you not remember your New Testament that says put aside what has gone before? Better yet, put aside both the Old and New Testaments that have been filtered by the church and religious leaders who use the Bible to exact religious control over you the way your other masters control you economically and politically. Carrying a Bible in one hand and a missile in the other is not doing God's work. An eye for an eye and tooth for a tooth will eventually make you blind and toothless."

Smiling, the old lady shouted, "amen."

As was his custom, Jesus looked at his spiral binder, opened it, read for a few seconds and started another homily. "The Old Testament abhors usury. In fact, it is categorized as an affront to God. Does that keep your nation's leaders who profess fealty to that book from allowing banks to engage in usury of the most obscene kind? Yet, they have no trouble decrying abortion or homosexuality. Why do they not stand against usury? You cannot be selective from the book. It either is or it isn't. And I say it isn't."

130

The crowd, who all, no doubt, either were or had been abused by lending institutions, applauded in unison. Now at least 500 strong, the applause roused Sheriff Dillon in his office. Knowing what was going on, he decided to go down to the park and survey the scene.

Again, enjoying the fact that he had the rapt attention of the crowd, Jesus continued his attacks on hypocrisy. "Do you good people really believe that Adam and Eve were created in the Garden of Eden and they were forbidden to eat from the tree of knowledge? The church wants you to believe that, because the church has always been afraid of knowledge. The church tells you religion will make you happy. So does whiskey, laughing gas and drugs. Yet, they tell you to avoid those evils. I say to you that religion can be evil, too. Stop worrying so much about your souls, and start worrying about the plight of your fellow man. As long as one man hungers, you should all hunger. How can the church set back and allow the chosen few to accumulate so much while the many cry for sustenance? As the great Upton Sinclair said, the supreme crime of the church today is that everywhere and in all its operations and influences it is on the side of ignorance of the mind. It banishes brains, it sanctifies stupidity and it canonizes incompetence."

131

"Why would you want to turn your mind over to an organization like that? Why would you support the church when it allows the wealthiest nation on earth to pile up an arsenal of ever more sophisticated weapons to kill the illiterate, the poor and the hungry across the globe? Does the church think you can kill ignorance, illness, poverty and hunger? Only love can tackle those afflictions, and you can never have that love when the church makes no demands for economic and social justice. If the church was doing its job, the ministers would all be in jail for fighting injustice. That is the way you serve God. Fight like hell against the machine that crushes justice."

The crowd, that was growing ever larger, included Sheriff Dillon, whom Jesus noticed was talking with the three F.B.I. agents who had slipped to the periphery of the crowd now. Jesus said, "there are those among you here who are Judases. They fear that I will teach you to emancipate yourselves from mental slavery. They are here to silence the prophet. They may not always kill the prophet, as the jails are full of those, like me, who refuse to bow before the tyranny of the ruling class. They do not realize that you can lock-up the body, but you cannot lock up the idea. I am here to save the earth, but these Judases are servants to those who are raping it."

As the Son of Thunder

The three F.B.I. agents and the sheriff felt intimidated by Jesus and the crowd that was hanging on his every word. Looking up toward the sun, Jesus raised his right hand in the air, palm facing the crowd. His words seemed to float through the air meekly but build in power as he said, "you are all victims of a cruel system that allocates the most to those who deserve it least. Yet, like sheep being led to the slaughter, you line up to serve your oppressors. You protest too meekly and willingly accept your fate. Samson accepted his fate, too, but thanks to a weak beam, not to a miracle, in a critical juncture of the temple, he saw the opportunity to make his oppressors pay the supreme price. He died along with them, but he brought his wrath upon those who had oppressed him. When will you people get some strength and do as Samson did? Stop throwing ice cubes at the sun and get a backbone. Do not go meekly to your fate – rage against the machine."

The sheriff and the agents beat a hasty retreat from the crowd, fearing that this rebel-rouser would incite it to acts against them. As they headed toward the sheriff's office, one of the agents was frantically talking on his cell phone, almost shouting, "send some help, send some help now. This guy is a terrorist."

133

CHAPTER 10
I AM THE ONE WHO DELIVERS THE BILL

Aaron had sit for almost an hour, captivated by Mary's tales of Jesus. He had also, at times, caught himself fantasizing about what it would be like to see her naked. He could not believe that after all these years of seemingly disinterest in sex that now, at 60, he was suddenly feeling his libido rejuvenated by this incredibly sexy woman who sat before him.

Mary let a devilish grin slowly slip across her lips. "Aaron, I appreciate your interest in the facts about this extraordinary man, and I am eager to share more with you, but you seem to have your mind on something else."

Aaron, somewhat embarrassed, replied, "I - I - I am sorry Mary. I- I- I.............."

Mary, not the least bit shy, said, "You seem unable to put an intelligible syllable together Aaron. I have seen that look before. It is a look with which I am very familiar. Men, and even some women I have been around, seem to get that look often in my presence. I know how to respond, but in recent days, I have not wanted to respond. It seems there are more important things in my life

134

now than earning a living through sex. Not that I would not enjoy sex, as it is my favourite recreational activity, as well as the way I pay the rent and put food on the table, but it seems that my life goes far beyond that now. I so want to make a difference and to reach out with compassion to those who cry in the darkness. I think I have always been a compassionate person, but I now feel my compassion has been recognized and validated by someone who has shown me a light that shines from afar and wraps me in its warmth."

Somewhat embarrassed, Aaron again fumbled for words. "I, I, I am so sorry. I beg your pardon. I do not mean to be crass or rude. I cannot explain what has come over me."

Mary, again showing that devilish grin that started in the middle of her mouth and slowly crept to the left side of her face, curling her moist, soft, full lips, almost laughed. "Aaron, do not apologize. It is a compliment to be desirable. Why should a woman be offended when a man lusts after her? The day will come when I am old, wrinkled and decrepit. Then, I will look fondly back on the time when men were aroused by me."

Aaron, this time without stuttering, said, "no matter how old or decrepit you may get, your kind

135

of beauty will prevail. It is not just a beauty of the flesh. It is a beauty of the soul."

"What a nice compliment. I am sure you have always done well with the ladies."

Aaron, somewhat proud of the fact that he might have impressed her as a man who once wowed the ladies, stood-up and replied, "well, I suppose I did alright, but not for a long time. I am afraid that bulb not only dimmed. It completely burned out."

Mary rose from the sofa and stood there in front of Aaron. She was breathing rhythmically, her voluptuous breasts rising precipitously, making her braless nipples seem to almost poke through the thin silk blouse she was wearing. Aaron felt the rise in his pants again.

Aaron was more than just sexually aroused. He looked at Mary as if she was a rose. There were thorns on the stem, but the blossom was beautiful. Those thorns would not be ignored by a society where judgemental arrogance pointed the finger of condemnation. Yet, Aaron could see past the thorns into her soul. The defects were not important, because he saw the nobility of a woman who had aroused passion within him that had been dead for so long. But this was more than passion,

136

As the Son of Thunder

it was a realization, a realization that from that moment forth, he would no longer be alone. Like the breaking morning sun that welcomes the day, an awareness rose in Aaron, freeing him from the depths of loneliness he had felt for so long, freeing him from any soulful fear of solitude. It was the beginning of love and the end of all that his life had been before. Yet, he knew it was hopeless. He was a weathered, rugged, worn-out old man, and she was a young, vibrant, alluring, beautiful woman.

Mary stood there, saying nothing, only looking at Aaron. Suddenly, she said in soft tone, "you have such an interesting face, Aaron. I really like it. I can see the pain of your life in it, and I can see the commitment of a man who refuses to bow before those who are hypocritical. You are a free man – a genuinely free man."

Aaron, becoming bolder now, moved a bit closer. "Would you want to kiss this face?"

Remembering an old line from a movie, she replied, "I said I like your face. I didn't say I wanted to kiss it."

Embarrassed at his boldness for thinking she might be interested, Aaron took a step back.

As the Son of Thunder

As he did, Mary moved forward so close he could feel her breath on his chin and said, "However, I could kiss it. I might like it."

Yes, this was passion, but it was passion borne of love at first sight for them both. It was un-hoped for, unexpected, unknown in so far as it was not a matter of conscious awareness. To their amazement, it was just there and it was overwhelming them.

Mary leaned forward, pressing her full, red, moist, supple lips passionately on Aaron's mouth. He gently parted his lips, as their tongues furiously sought one another. Blotting out all the extemporaneous things about them, as the passion and blissfulness boiled up from deep within, their minds seemed to float from their bodies as they both felt they were soaring overhead, looking down at the passionate lovers harmoniously wrapped in each other's arms.

Reaching down to the bottom of her loose blouse, Mary slowly and deliberately pulled it up over her head. Aaron, having not made love in years, felt like an adolescent getting ready for his first real sexual experience. He did not know whether he should be removing his clothes or helping Mary remove hers. It became a moot point

138

when Mary simply unbuttoned her skirt and it fell to the floor about her ankles. Braless, her huge globular breasts heaved up and down as she gently removed her panties, exposing a dark, full bush that went far onto her thighs on each side, and a tiny trail of black hair rose all the way up to her navel. Aaron thought how refreshing it was to see a woman who did not bow before Madison Avenue's idea of what sexy was. She was a natural woman and proud of it.

Kissing him as she removed his shirt and unbuttoned his pants, Aaron felt his manhood, seemingly struggling to free itself from his briefs. It got some help from Mary, who removed his briefs as she fell to her knees and devoured his manhood in one giant swallow. Aaron stood there in ecstasy, staring at the ceiling, as Mary worked feverously back and forth. Aaron's breathing quickened and he felt himself ready to explode. Fearful that his excitement would make him spend all his energy without plunging into Mary's wetness, he gently pulled her up from her knees and found her mouth again. He pressed her ever closer, feeling that he wanted to melt their bodies into one. They lingered in a long, passionate kiss. He lowered her onto the floor and began to nibble on her breasts as she moaned in delight. He kissed his way down her ribs and stomach, stopping to

139

blow gently on her coal black pubic hair, tracing it with his tongue from her navel to the top of the opening to her delightful womanhood. He worked his way between her legs and she placed her hands on his silvery hair, pushing his face deeper and deeper into her opening. Wrapping her legs around his head, she tried to put his whole face inside her, pushing and thrusting at the same time. She wanted all of him.

Finally, exhausted from pushing and thrusting, she muttered, "give it to me Aaron, please give it to me hard."

Aaron arose from between her legs like the Greek God Poseidon rising from the depths of the sea. His member was pulsating with hardness as he slid it into her. Making deep thrusts as Mary moaned, they were both lost in the ecstasy of the moment. Rhythmically meeting his ever thrust, Mary breathed heavily and cried aloud for his seed. "I need it! I need it! Dump it deep in me, Aaron. I want you inside me. I want your seed."

Pounding hard on her, Aaron was making guttural sounds with each thrust. Then Mary felt the pulsating rhythm of Aaron's member as he exploded deep within her, letting out a deep sigh of relief.

140

As the Son of Thunder

To make sure she got every drop of Aaron's seed, she wrapped her legs around him and pulled him in deeper. Breathing heavily, she smiled and said, "not bad for an old man who thought he was through with sex."

Aaron, as proud as an adolescent who had just scored his first conquest, smiled, dismounted, turned and lay beside Mary still breathing heavily as his member collapsed in exhaustion.

Aaron put out his left arm and Mary nestled into it and cuddled up to his chest, wrapping her left arm around him, as if she wanted to hold onto him forever. They both realized that time is too slow for those who wait, and too swift for those who fear. They were rejoicing in new found love and passion, and they would make a short time into an eternity.

Suddenly, Aaron realized that his age was not a barrier to this woman. The great sex they just had might never occur again, but it would not matter to either one of them. When love is accompanied by deep intimacy it is indeed the highest level of human experience. They had both attained a glimpse of the rapture, and it had nothing to do with the Bible. This was a rejoicing in the union of two beings and there were no limitations.

141

Aaron turned to Mary and said, "I had stopped looking for so long. I never dreamed there was someone like you out there. You were just a name back in New York City, a name connected with a dead friend. My friend gets killed, and because of that, I found you. How ironic that it took his death for me to find you. I suppose there is some truth to that old adage that what seems bad in the past, can lead to good in the future. I just hate I had to lose Dixon to find you. But, I assure you someone will pay for Dixon's death and for the disappearance of your friend, and I am going to be the one who delivers the bill."

As the Son of Thunder

CHAPTER 11
THE WRATH OF AARON ADAMS

Putting aside their concerns about finding Jesus when they found each other, Mary and Aaron spent the night in peaceful bliss wrapped in each others arms, except for the two times they awakened to again satisfy their carnal instincts. The next morning, Aaron found himself singing in the shower with Mary, as they fondled and kissed under the warm spray that seemed to bathe them in an afterglow of harmonious tranquility. Aaron, could not get over his new found libido, as in the shower, he again rose to the occasion and fornicated with ferocious intensity, letting out a scream as he planted his seed deep inside Mary once again.

Mary, laughing out-loud, said, "for a man who was complaining about his lack of libido, I think you must have undoubtedly been storing it up for one night of wild sex."

Aaron, still feeling like an adolescent, replied "baby, I am a stick of dynamite wrapped in a veil of mischief."

Mary, her eyes twinkling with merriment, said, "sweetheart, you certainly exploded like a stick of

143

dynamite again and again and ...."

Before she could finish her last "again," Aaron wrapped her in his arms and pressed his lips to hers, cutting her off in mid-sentence. And there it was, that stick of dynamite was on the rise, ready to explode once more. Sweeping her up in his arms, he carried her to the bed, both of them still dripping wet. Desire overwhelmed them, and they floated off into that blissful serenity found, not just in passionate ardour, but in love between two people who have become one.

Exhausted, but euphoric, as Mary slept, Aaron gazed upon her beauty. It was not the classic beauty as promulgated by the Madison Avenue gurus who brainwashed men and women both into believing that you were worthless if you were not slim and perfectly proportioned. Mary's beauty was much deeper. Aaron surveyed her, starting at her feet. The brightly painted toe nails were perfectly manicured and the big toes on both feet had a slight bend to them, no doubt from years of wearing high heals. Her calves were muscular and full.

As his eyes moved up to her thighs, Aaron noticed a small scar on her left leg. Then there was that magnificently thick, full, coal black pubic

144

hair that spread out all over her lower abdomen. Within that patch of hair was the loveliness of her womanhood that was long and widely gapped as it worked its way downward. Aaron could see a tinge of his white man batter that lay glistening on the dark hair.

Her stomach was not fat, nor was it washboard flat. It protruded slightly but seductively, almost inviting a person to rest a head on the softness. And again, that coal dark hair made a narrow trail as it worked its way up to her deeply indented navel.

Looking between his legs, Aaron felt a rise again, but he was too engrossed in surveying Mary's body to do anything about it. Yet, he instinctively reached down and put his right hand on it, slightly pulling back and forth to relieve the almost aching tension.

As he pulled back and forth on his member, his eyes concentrated on her breasts – huge orbs that had long, erect, protruding nipples that seemed to cry for attention from a wet, darting tongue and warm succulent mouth. Breathing heavily now, he looked at her moderately thick neck that rose to a magnificent chin with a very small dimple right in the middle that was only slightly discernable.

145

Her face seemed as if it had been brush stroked by a master artist. There were faint laugh lines and a few crow's feet around her eyes. And those eyes, they were closed now, but even the lids were beautiful, soft and dark, harbouring the tranquility of a deep sleep that had arrested her beauty.

Pulling harder on his member, the bed began to shake and Aaron started to moan louder. Opening her eyes with a smile slowing creeping across her lips at the same time, Mary, engrossed at Aaron's need for relief, said, "don't waste that, I need my morning protein."

Sweeping down on his member in one motion and gobbling it up like a starving desert sojourner who had found a bubbling brook in an oasis, Aaron exploded with a thunderous roar that hit the back of Mary's mouth like a tsunami coming ashore.

Lying between Aaron's legs and looking up, Mary seemed incredibly pleased with herself. "Damn, you really know how to greet a girl in the morning."

Looking down at her, Aaron, once again surprised at his new found virility, could only whisper, "I may be dying."

146

As the Son of Thunder

Neither one of them had used the word love, but it was there. It was easy to see that morning simply because they were not telling each other how much in love they were. Aaron was fixing eggs and bacon, and Mary was sitting there smiling but half asleep. Still naked, Aaron's member had finally dropped to less than half-mast. Mary, exhausted but showing total satisfaction in her demeanour, began to giggle as she watched Aaron preparing breakfast naked. Any objective observer could tell they were in love.

The domesticity of the situation made Aaron look about the kitchen and survey all that was before him. Mary, sitting naked at the kitchen table, smiling up at him, and the smell of the bacon and eggs was a heavenly delight.

Long ago he had loved a woman who had penetrated his soul, but she had left him in the throes of desperate loneliness that had plunged him into an abyss of misery for years, but Mary had created something out of nothing. She was the master designer who had put his old world to sleep and brought a supreme delicacy that penetrated to the depths of his being. Why had it taken him so long to find her? He came here, not even looking, because he had given up hope, but love had reached out and warmly embraced him.

147

Love protects, trusts, hopes and perseveres. Aaron and Mary were at peace with one another. Still, unable to fathom the immensity of what had occurred, Aaron placed the plates of bacon and eggs on the table, sat down and pensively said, "Mary, you realize our age difference? I am afraid I can't perform like last night and this morning very often."

"Aaron, a woman can get sex on any street-corner, but we aren't talking about sex. The sex was great, but I got more than that last night, and I hope you feel the same way. I can live without sex, but I need love. Without love, you only exist, not live."

Reaching over and taking her left hand in his right hand, Aaron smiled. Then, letting go of her hand, the two of them began to eat, the clanging of the forks on their plates penetrating the silence. They sit quietly in loving, blissful serenity.

Mary penetrated the silence in her soft, melodious voice. "I have held many others before, but never like I held you last night. It is as if my body inhales you and I quiver with bliss. I was consumed by a raging fire, and I sit here in quiet repose still simmering. It is a flame that cannot ever be extinguished. My heart belongs to you. I

148

am peaceful and complete."

Aaron, consumed with wonder at how this beautiful, young woman could feel that way about an old, worn-out man replied to her stoically. "My soul was lost. I was not even chasing happiness any longer. I gave up on it long ago as weary hours merged into weary days, weary months and weary years. I was consumed by darkness, but my long night has ended and the way onward lies open in glorious splendour that bathes me in light at long last."

Sooner or later people begin to understand that love is more than rhyming verses, more than passionate kisses on the silver screen and more than descriptive tales on printed pages. People begin to realize that love is here and now, and that it must be grabbed, held and cherished. Love is a promise that is always kept, a fortune that can never be depleted, a seed that can flourish in the most unlikely places. This radiance never fades, rather it brightens and glows in mysterious joy all about those whom it encompasses. These two sit across the kitchen table from one another, flying without wings. They soared to heights they had never imagined.

Not having a change of clothes, Mary graciously

149

washed Aaron's clothes while he sat in a terry cloth robe that had been left by one of Mary's men friends. Seemingly unashamed of having it, she explained to Aaron that her old life was over now, but that she would never hide or be ashamed of what she had been, because Jesus had taught her there were far greater sins than selling your body for money. It was then that she started to share more tales of this man who had changed her life, beginning where she had left off the previous evening before she and Aaron were overwhelmed by their passion.

More of Mary's Tales of Jesus and His Teachings

When the F.B.I. agents in Woodbury begged for help in combating what they felt was a terrorist in their midst, the U.S. government sent a crack team of operatives into the small New Jersey town to protect the U.S. homeland from what they considered a subversive individual who was encouraging the people to commit acts of rebellion against the government. This humble man had no personal weapons, other than the power of his words to arouse people to question their government. He had no mighty army equipped by corporate defence industrialists to carry out attacks. He had no monetary assistance from supporters. Yet, the government feared him.

150

As the Son of Thunder

Being somewhat bound by the dying idea that its citizens were guaranteed freedom of speech, the three F.B.I. agents and the special government team had to wait for the right moment to eliminate this threat to authority. It was imperative that this nascent movement to eliminate fear not be allowed to take root and spread beyond the boundaries of the small New Jersey town. This was the job of these government thugs – to protect the people from anyone who encouraged them to question the motives of those in power.

Meanwhile, as the days went on, Jesus continued his sojourns, meeting people individually and appearing at public gatherings in the downtown area, Mary and Dixon always by his side.

One morning, as he, Mary and Dixon sat in the diner, a group of ministers came over and asked if they could talk with him for awhile. Pulling up three chairs, the group seemed intent on challenging Jesus' knowledge of the Bible.

The youngest minister, who was immaculately attired in a brown, tailor-made suit, fidgeted with his finely manicured nails as he said, "we hear that you had the nerve to say that it was the sound of trumpets that brought down the walls of Jericho rather than God's divine intervention."

151

Jesus, looking a bit rumpled in his Wal-Mart bought clothes when compared to the finely dressed representatives of the church, replied by asking a question. "Where were you educated my good man?"

"I don't know what that has to do with the question, but I was educated at the University of North Carolina and Duke Divinity School."

Jesus, smiling now, seemed to be relishing the moment. "I was not educated in the finest schools. I was educated with hard work, like so many of my contemporaries. I learned to do things with my hands. As a carpenter, I learned how to calculate and measure from a father who could neither read or write, but he could out-figure a trained mathematician, because he learned by experience. I was taught to never accept what I am told at face-value, but to search for the truth myself, rather than depending on someone else to do my thinking for me. I am not degrading your education. I am sure you had many fine purveyors of knowledge, but I am just as certain that the majority of the professors at the institutions you attended did not tell you that you should believe in fairy tales. If you told a professor you believed in Mother Goose, he would laugh you out of the classroom."

Now, perturbed at what he saw as an evasion of the question, the minister said rather curtly, "you are not answering the question."

Jesus smiled slightly and replied, "but I am answering the question. You, as an educated man, believe that God responded to the needs of the Israelite army by tumbling the walls of Jericho? Yet, you cannot accept the plausible explanation of sound being used to create cracks in the wall, and then, that these cracks grew until the walls eventually crumbled? How can you call yourself an educated man? Did you not study the basics of science? God is an idea more than a being. We are each capable of being God. Man has a brain, if he uses it properly, he has no need of God's miracles. He can perform his own."

One of the other ministers, a man of about 50 with a pompadour hairstyle that had not a single hair out-of-place, said curtly, "so, I suppose Jesus never raised anyone from the dead?"

Jesus replied matter-of-factly, "there you go again. Do you believe in fairy tales or in scientific facts? People come back from death today all the time, without any Godly intervention? What made the incident of raising a dead man any different from a doctor resuscitating a person today?"

153

The minister had no answer, but as he was struggling for one, the third minister, a balding man of perhaps 40, interjected, "so, I suppose Elijah was not carried away to heaven either."

Obviously, loving the intellectual exercise of a lively discussion, Jesus never faltered in his response. "I am sure you have watched magicians perform. One even made the Statue of Liberty disappear. Making Elijah appear to ascend to heaven would be relatively easy for a man who could make the Statute of Liberty disappear. Aaron changing his rod into a serpent was as simple as pulling a rabbit from a hat. What does it take for individuals to realize that the real God is within each man's brain, only some of us learn to use it better than others. I am not here to dispel belief in God. I am here to let humanity know that they are all Gods, all capable of greater miracles than ever portrayed in the Bible. Put aside self-interest, pride, the insidiousness of greed and all things are possible. Do you not think that if this nation would turn its weapons of mass-destruction into ploughshares that the most destructive disease known to man, poverty, could be swept into the dust-bin of history?"

All three were appalled at the questioning of the very tenants upon which their faith was based. The

154

three of them could muster no credible response, but the youngest one said, "you sir are an abomination, an affront to the Christian faith."

Jesus, always eager for verbal sparring, had an immediate response. "I know what the real abomination is. It is an abomination to use fear to scare little children into believing that God is vengeful. What kind of God would destroy the children of Sodom and Gomorrah while punishing the sins of the parents? What kind of God would punish Lot's wife by turning her to a pillar of salt, because she was compassionate enough to look back and fret for the suffering of the people doomed by a vengeful God? What kind of God would take the lives of the first born of Egypt as retribution for the evil of their parents? Fear of God is a powerful tool used by the exploiters to keep the exploited in bondage. I am here to free people from fear – the fear of a vengeful God, the fear of the rich, the fear of the powerful and the fear of those who proclaim themselves the interpreters of God's word. There is one thing for those who enslave people's minds, bodies and spirits to fear – my words. Make no mistake, I am not here to lead a revolution. I am not a liberator, because only people can liberate themselves. I am nothing more than a catalyst, a catalyst to awaken a sleeping giant, the American people."

155

Disgusted and appalled by what they had heard from this purported holy man, the three got up. The oldest one said in parting, "you will rue the day you attacked the sanctity of the church."

As they turned to leave, Jesus said to Mary and Dixon, purposefully loud enough for the departing ministers to hear, "and they shall rue the day they used the church for personal gain and self-aggrandizement."

Jesus, Mary and Dixon got up immediately and all three walked over to the cashier, a man of perhaps 50, with a white apron on that covered a rather rotund belly. Dixon had learned after several days with Jesus that he or Mary were expected to pay the bill, as Jesus was a man of no financial means whatsoever. As the cashier counted out Dixon's change, he looked directly at Jesus. Almost whispering, he said, "you should be careful of antagonizing those three men. They are three of the most powerful men in this community."

Jesus replied, "Do you fear them?"

The cashier, still in a whispering tone, said, "I own this place, and one word from them to their parishioners and my business is history."

Dixon and Mary looked at each other with a facial expression that seemed to say, "here we go. This man is about to get a lesson in fear."

Jesus very calmly replied to the owner, "what is your name?"

"I am Tom Horner."

"Tom, do you have a family?"

"Yes, I have a wife and three children from 8 to 17."

Jesus, as always, warming to the occasion, leaned in a bit closer and he, himself, whispered. "Tom, you have a responsibility to put food on the table for your family. So, I can understand why you fear those who would take food from the mouths of your children. Yet, if you were a slave and knew that you could break free from your shackles by enduring the pain of hammering them lose, would you be willing to endure the agony? Remember, it is better to experience the pain of life than not to experience life at all. He who lives in fear, teaches his children to live in fear. Every man deserves freedom, but most men line up to be slaves without even realizing it. Be careful that you are not one of those who lines up for chains."

157

Mary and Dixon could not help but smile at each other, because once again Jesus had left a man speechless. The three of them walked from the restaurant, as the owner stared off into space with a dumbfounded look on his face, but it was obvious that he was thinking about what Jesus had said to him.

As the three of them turned to stroll toward the park, that familiar black sedan pulled up to the curb with the white haired man driving. Right behind him was a black SUV with three other men in it. On the passenger side of the sedan, one of the agents flung open the door, blocking the sidewalk. He quickly lunged in front of Jesus, whipped out his badge and said, "Agent Carter again, we need to talk to you."

Behind Jesus, Mary and Dixon, the three men from the SUV very quickly blocked any chance they had for retreat. The white haired agent had gotten out of the car and walked up to Jesus. He quickly removed his badge from his inside coat pocket, holding it up in front of Jesus as if he was a king and it was his crown. As one of the men from the other car came up beside him, the agent said, "I am Agent Shaw, and this is Mr. Helpern, Special Agent with the NSA. He needs to have a few words with you."

As the Son of Thunder

Completely unimpressed, Jesus replied, "What business do I have with the F.B.I. or the National Security Agency?"

Agent Shaw replied, "Maybe none, but it is up to us to determine whether you do or not. I suggest you come along with us."

Unperturbed, as a curious crowd began to gather around them, Jesus turned to the crowd and said, "this is an example of what happens when a nation lives in fear. These men are the idea police. You see, ideas are weapons, and the U.S. government fears ideas more than it fears anything else."

Obviously upset at the courageous boldness of this man, Agent Helpern, with a look of disgust on his face, leaned in close to Jesus, looking directly into his eyes. "Listen you son-of-bitch, we aren't messing around. You better get in the car and come with us."

Jesus smiled and said, "you men probably went to work for the government with good intentions. You might have even thought you could change the system. You fail to realize that you don't change the system, the system changes you. The only real change comes through revolution of the oppressed. You are all oppressed but too stupid to

159

realize it. You are being buried alive but do not see those who are shovelling dirt over your graves, because you are blinded by the propaganda that keeps you in chains. You, like 99% of the population need to free yourself from mental slavery. Your government thinks, like so many other governments in the past, that it can silence the voice of the prophets. You can lock me up. You can torture me. You can kill me, but you will never snuff out the ideals for which I stand. I am a one man revolution that will not be stayed."

The white-haired agent, Shaw, stepped between Helpern and Jesus. As he did, Jesus turned his back on the agents of despair and addressed the gathering crowd. "These men represent a government that is your oppressor. You have all been tricked into fear, so that you will fight perpetual wars of mass genocide on enemies that do not exist, so corporations can reap obscene profits. Make no mistake, war is big business in America. The biggest enemy is not without. It is within. All exterior enemies are created to justify the advancement of the military-industrial complex that uses fear to keep you bound in patriotic servitude. There is but one way to end this calamity of control. The masses must band together, rise up and demand justice. Remember that dissent is the highest form of patriotism."

As the Son of Thunder

"Since 9/11, you have all been prisoners of state terror and patriotic propaganda. Most of you have not been in a prison with bars, because you are you own jailers. The government does not have to incarcerate most of you, because you incarcerate yourselves with ignorance."

As the crowd broke into applause, Shaw whispered to Helpern, "this situation is getting out of hand. Leave him alone. We need to get out of here before the situation escalates. We will pick him up when there is no one around."

When the agents went to their cars and pulled off, the crowd broke out in more applause. However, Jesus was more contemplative. "They retreat to lick their wounds. Yet, make no mistake. They will be back. It is part of the golden rule. And what is the golden rule? It is not the one you were taught in Sunday School. Simply put, the golden rule is that those with the gold rule. Those men serve those with the gold."

As Jesus started to leave, a blind man in the back of the crowd came forward and said, "if you are who you say you are, cure my blindness."

Jesus touched the much shorter man's head and said, "if I was that powerful, why would I just cure

161

your blindness. Why wouldn't I just eliminate blindness as one of man's afflictions, so there would be no more blindness for anyone. Man has the ability to eliminate all afflictions, but the problem is your government had rather spend money on bombs and bullets than on what its citizens genuinely need. What a wonderful paradise this country could be if the money spent on weapons was used to fight disease and poverty, rather than on weapons to subject all humanity to the evil of a system based on greed. The great masquerade of evil cloaked in government propaganda plays havoc with the genuine needs of the people."

Rather than being appalled that he was not healed, the blind man reached up to touch Jesus' face. "I see, not your face, not the sunshine that I long to gaze upon, but I can see with my heart. I see the possibilities offered by your sage counsel. I shall no longer linger in chains, hoping for change from a society that reveres the status-quo. I shall work to make others with sight, but who are still blind, see the possibilities of the world of which you speak."

"Friend, it is hard to free fools from the chains they revere. Today, you are no longer a fool, because you have cut the chains that bind you."

162

Dixon turned to Jesus and said, "there are those who would say you did not perform a miracle here, but I say to you that what you have just done for this man is indeed a miracle. You lifted up his spirit and made him see that true miracles are performed by men who care for one another, not by some deity on high."

Jesus, smiling, motioned for Dixon and the crowd to follow him toward the park. He turned to Dixon with a contemplative look on his face. "Dixon, you are beginning to perceive what true miracles are. Revolution is not a trail of roses. It is a road fraught with danger. It is a fight to the death between the past and the future. I perform no miracles. I only plant the seeds from which mighty trees can soar. I can reach out to a thousand people, but only a few will understand my message. Yet, if those few reach out to a thousand and another few understand their message and reach out to another thousand, the seeds of rebellion will be planted and a mighty forest will grow from that one initial seed."

Mary, as she walked with Jesus, contemplated all he had taught her in the few days she had known him. Her belief in self-sacrifice was strengthened. She had grown to despise the kind of existence that clings to the miserly trifles of self

163

interest. Mary had never felt so free in her life. Yet, she realized that the weak and timid would never be free. Freedom required work and sacrifice from those who longed to be loosened from their chains.

Looking at Jesus as he strode through the park, making his way toward the picnic table that served as his podium, Mary noticed the sun's rays forming a kaleidoscope of colours about his head. It was as if a thousand graces were diffusing all about him. His measured, smooth strides showed no signs of haste, and as he mounted the picnic table the sun's rays seemed to dance about his head. This was more than a man. Mary thought of what one of her favourite teachers had said in class many years ago, "men do not shape destiny. Destiny produces the man for the hour." Was this the hour? Was this the man?

Jesus looked out at the crowd that had now grown to at least 300 and began his discourse. "I have been accosted by authorities today. The word authorities has a sinister meaning, because it gives a few the right to impugn the rights of the many. This nation's leaders speak of human rights as if it has a monopoly on righteousness. I say to you, what moral authority do they have to speak of human rights? They use torture, but simply call it

164

by a different name. If you fight torture with torture, how does that elevate you above those whom you call your enemies?"

"This is a nation where the billionaire and the beggar are supposed to have equal rights. Is there any among you foolish enough to believe that? This is a country that condemns genocide, but has never come to terms with its own attempts to exterminate its native population. The minorities, whether black or brown, are scorned, exploited and humiliated. The corporations of this nation are nothing but modern day feudal lords who traffic in the labour they extract from those who must bow in supplication to receive their sustenance. Your government conducts global terror through both overt and covert means by condoning the monopolies of wealth and power that enslave whole continents to corporate malfeasance in the name of liberty. This nation glorifies greed as an enviable trait. Yet, all of you sanction these abominations by your silence."

Jesus, again, noticed the three ministers from the diner among the crowd. Pointing directly at them with an accusatory right index finger, he said, "look among you for those who deceive. Ask yourself what you are being taught from the church pulpits all across this land."

165

All three stood defiantly and the older one shouted, "you are blasphemous. How dare you question the integrity of the church."

Addressing his remarks directly at the three, Jesus pointed both his hands toward the front of his chest. "I am blasphemous? Should the church be engaging in a spiritual reign of terror over people, threatening them with earthly and eternal punishment in order to make them cower in fear? Do your words of intimidation not bring tyranny to the very idea of a loving God? When people are called to follow a loving Jesus, they are proclaimed free of all human rules, everything which presumes, burdens or causes worry and torment of conscience. People are released from the arrogance of those who keep them in bondage. Rather than preaching against the sins of the flesh, the church should preach against the sins of arrogance, selfishness, war, famine and greed. How can you preach against abortion, then allow those born into poverty to be denied healthcare or a roof over their heads? How can you decry homosexuality, but then preach about the power of love. What is wrong with a man loving a man, or a woman loving a woman? Love is love, pure and simple. You condemn and judge without remembering that admonition to judge not, lest you be judged."

166

The youngest of the three ministers shouted above the raucous roar of the crowd, "this is a nation dedicated to liberty. You, sir, are preaching anarchy."

Jesus was obviously delighted with the man's response, because it led logically to his next admonition of the three. "Like so many people who represent the status quo, you use words to mask evil. Your government doesn't call water-boarding torture, rather it is enhanced interrogation techniques. Yet, no matter how you cloud it with colourful language – torture is still torture. For some, the word liberty may mean the right of all men to reach their full-potential as a by-product of their labour, while for some men, it simply means the freedom to enslave others to a system of bondage based on greed. Just because you use the word liberty, does not mean someone else doesn't look on it as tyranny. Do you believe those who suffer from this nation's bombs and bullets think you are bringing them liberty or are bringing them tyranny? The answer should be obvious. Any church that sits idly by while a nation engages is these acts of tyranny is as guilty as those who order the bombs dropped. To sin by silence, neglect or ignorance is a cowardly act that does great disservice to the very ideals for which the church is supposed to stand."

167

As the crowd roared with approval, the three simply shook their heads as they, again, walked away, dumbfounded by the remarkable insights offered by this man.

Still not finished, as the three were walking away, Jesus said, "they leave, not to think about what I have said, but to lick their wounds and plot the demise of one who challenges their authority. They will condemn me to one and all. Yet, it does not matter, because history will absolve me."

Dixon noticed the three of them meet just outside the park entrance with the three F.B.I. agents, the three N.S.A. agents and Sheriff Dillon. Obviously, they were not discussing the weather. It looked even more sinister when a black limousine pulled up and Agent Shaw, Agent Helpern and the eldest minister all got into the back seat with a man clothed in elaborate purple vestments. This was, no doubt, a high ranking Catholic Church official.

The car pulled off and the rest of the men walked away with Sheriff Dillon. The sun went behind a cloud and Dixon thought that it was a prophetic sign of the darkness that was about to shroud his new found friend in a cacophony of tyranny wrought by those who feared him.

As the Son of Thunder

Continuing his teachings, Jesus spotted a man whom he knew in the crowd. Looking down at him, he said, "I see my friend Matthew is among you. He has journeyed many places, many times throughout this land and other distance lands with me to bring the truth to those who are fed a steady diet of lies. Come up here Matthew and stand by my side. I am going to use you to illustrate a point about why we should not be judgemental."

Matthew was not a handsome man by any means. His head was long and narrow. His ears were large and the lobes flopped about like those on an elephant. His hair was dark and seemed to be piled on his head rather than merely growing from the scalp. His cheek bones were high and prominent on his emaciated looking face. He had an incredibly large nose that had a pronounced bend toward the right eye. His dark eyebrows were thick and almost reached his long scraggily sideburns on each side of his face. And what a face. It was sallow, cadaverous, shrunken, wrinkled, leathery and looked as if it had fought a battle with a meat cleaver and lost. This man could easily have been an exhibit at Ripley's *Believe It or Not Museum*. Yet, there was a quiet dignity about him as he mounted the picnic table to stand beside his friend. The crowd was aghast at his appearance, and several people actually gasped in

169

fear at this hideous looking creature.

Jesus wrapped his arms around him and pulled him to his chest, embracing him warmly. Turning Matthew to face the crowd, Jesus pointed at the tattered left breast pocket of Matthew's shirt, then he removed an empty cigarette pack from the pocket. He spoke softy to the crowd. "My friend will tell you about addictions and how we are all addicted one way or another." Jesus stepped down, sit on the picnic table bench, made a motion to Dixon with his right hand as if he was writing something. Dixon took it as a que to hand him a fountain pen. Jesus tore the cellophane wrapper from the cigarettes and jotted something down on the inside of the wrapper. He handed it up to Matthew, who held it up to the crowd.

As he held it high above his head, this scraggily, unkempt man began his story. "These represent just one of my addictions. I carry it as a reminder that I have no right to judge others who are addicted, because we are all addicts of one kind or another. I was a slave to cigarettes for nearly 50 years. I fell victim at an early age to the demons of corporate America who hook young people through manipulative advertising on one of the most addictive drugs in the world. Yet, they get away with it because of their power. It is perfectly

170

alright for them to peddle their drugs all over the U.S.A., but the dealer of drugs on the street corner is locked up as a menace to society. Who is the greater menace – the corporations that sell their poison to 80 million people a year, or those who sell their drugs to 8 million people a year? The answer should be obvious, but the power of the corporation prevents any of their CEO'S from spending time in jail for drug dealing."

"Looking at me in my emaciated condition would not make you think that I once was grossly overweight. Yet, I was addicted to food filled with additives that addict you as surly as any drug you could buy on the streets. Again, that is o.k., because it is a corporation that is addicting you. So, the next time you point the finger of condemnation at those suffering from the ravages of drug addiction, think about your own addictions. Whether it is addiction to food, to cigarettes, to alcohol, to sex, to television or to any of the multitude of things that entrap us in a prison of the mind – always be aware that none of us is truly free of addiction."

Jesus mounted the table again, stood beside his friend and said, "this is a man of courage, who was not just addicted to cigarettes, but to a host of other drugs. Every day of his life, he must fight

171

a lonely battle to keep himself clean. He has been by my side periodically for years. Many look on him with disdain. I look on him with admiration. Here is a man who faces demons every day of his life and fights them with determination. He also fights against ignorance that clouds the minds of those who fail to see that each person is master of his fate and captain of his soul. Too many of us do not realize that courage is not a lack of fear, rather it is the lack of the ability to face fear. My day of reckoning will soon be at hand, as it has been at hand many times before. Am I afraid? Yes, he who does not fear the pain of death is foolish. However, which do I fear more – death or living? It often takes more courage to live than to die, just as it takes more courage to love than to hate. The measure of love is what one is willing to give up for it. I have given my life many times."

Matthew stepped down from the picnic table just as Jesus said the word "life." He hung his head low, as if he knew something terrible was going to happen. Jesus reached down and picked up his spiral binder, as the crowd stood in silence, contemplating what he had just said.

Dixon and Mary pulled Matthew to the side as Jesus continued to speak, and asked him how he came to know this extraordinary man.

172

As the Son of Thunder

Matthew replied that he had know him for what seemed an eternity. He had been with him in many places to spread rebellion of one type or another. He had come late to Woodbury Creek, because he had been in a Carey, North Carolina jail.

He was adamant that he had never met a more forceful man. Jesus' sincerity, his devotion to humanity and his determination to do all he could to save it from subjugation to the rich and powerful was unparalleled. He could not attest to his divinity, but he sensed that he was as close to a God as any man he had ever seen. Yet, he never claimed any divinity. The closest he came to doing that was calling himself the son-of-man.

Jesus, looking down at the crowd, pointed to the sky and said, "do not look up there for heaven. You all have heaven in your grasp right here. The problem is that there are a few who want to get all the bounty for themselves while denying it to you. When the poor take things to feed their families, it is called looting. When the multi-national corporations control the market place and allow people to starve, it is not looting. It is free enterprise. You must all understand that if there is one person who is hungry, then there is no freedom. Freedom also means economic security and independence."

173

"There is no such thing as a little freedom. You are either free or you are not. How free can you be when you depend on a corporation for your job, for your education, for your food, for your transportation, for your healthcare and for your retirement?"

Someone in the front of the crowd, drinking from a plastic water bottle, shouted, "yeah, down with corporations, especially the oil companies who are raping us at the pump."

Jesus looked down at him and said, "so, you think the oil companies are raping you at the pump? Why don't you try walking, car-pooling, or bicycling? Why don't you spend your vacations at home? Believe me, I am not here to defend corporations. However, it is within your power to bring them to their knees, if you all banned together collectively to attack those who keep you in bondage. I notice you have a plastic bottle of water made by the same corporation that also addicts you to sugar-laden soft drinks. You have any idea what you are paying per gallon or litre for water you can get out of the tap? About 10 times what you are paying for gasoline. You probably buy ink for a computer. Do the simple math and you will find that you are paying about $5,000 a gallon or about $1200 a litre. You are a slave to the

174

corporations, and simply line up to let them rape you without realizing it. You attack corporations without realizing that you are supporting the very thing which you are attacking."

"I am here to shame not just you my good man, but all of you. I am appalled at how people actually think this nation allows you freedom. How many of you live without a computer, a television, a radio, a cell phone, electricity or the other multitude of things that you are convinced bring you happiness? Those things require money, and money is at the centre of all things you consider good. Even the church requires you to pay an admission charge by passing a collection plate at services while the ministers tell you that God loves a cheerful giver. You support a government that encourages wasteful consumption, so that your corporate masters can amass huge profits. Yet, when all the trees have been cut down, when all the animals have been hunted, when all your waters have been polluted, when all your air is unsafe to breath, only then will you discover that you cannot eat money. Greed is the beast that is devouring this land, and each and every person is a victim of its insidious, veracious appetite that consumes everything in its path. The promise and hope of a nation is being laid waste to feed this beast."

175

As the Son of Thunder

As always, when Jesus was on a roll, his rhetoric picked up in pace and you could sense a smug satisfaction as he felt he was reaching at least a few of the people. He knew that sowing the seeds of rebellion in a few might lead to a multiplying effect that could help stay the oppressive nature of a society that was destroying itself through the acquiescence to tyranny by those being governed.

"I see so many young people here today. They live in a country that extols the virtues of progress. But, is all progress good? And is it really progress? Many of these young people have probably never been to a grocery store that uses paper bags. Yet, they are told that plastic is better. Is it better to pollute the environment with plastic that lasts for thousands of years, or with paper that will decompose? Is it better for us physically to ride an elevator or walk up stairs? Is it better to get into a gas-guzzling machine to ride to the grocery store or to walk? Is it better to wash cloth baby diapers or to pile up disposal diapers in land-fills all over the country? Is it better to use a dryer that gobbles up expensive energy to dry your clothes or to hang them on a clothes line? Look at what you have become, courtesy of your government, which collaborates with your corporate masters to enslave you."

176

"I am here to show you that greed has made this nation an abomination. So many of you call yourselves Christians, but do nothing to sanctify yourselves before the God you profess to love. Some of the most compassionate people I have met on my journeys call themselves atheists, whereas many of the cruellest people proudly proclaim their fealty to God. Belief in God does not make you good, it can often blind you to the evil that is carried out in the name of God. How can a nation that proclaims itself righteous allow homeless people to roam the streets when there are millions of foreclosed houses sitting empty? How can the ministers of churches allow their pews to be empty in the evenings when the church could be used to offer shelter to those who have none? Are they not like the very people who turned away a woman named Mary who bore the holy child?

Many in the crowd were obviously appalled that this man would question their faith. Some started to wander away, shaking their heads, while others strained to hear more from a man who seemed to get to the very heart of the ills that plagued an economically and morally bankrupt society. As many left, others flocked into the park. At the park entrance, the three ministers had returned with several members of their congregations and were encouraging people to stay away from a man who

177

was going to lead them to eternal damnation.

Jesus, watching a few people leave who could not tolerate the truth, continued with his attack on greed. "You are told that greed is not only natural, but that it is good. I say to you that greed only gives the crumbs to the poor while providing the wealthy with a table of plenty. How can that be good? The rich want the poor and the middle class to fight for their crumbs. How can that be good? This nation could feed the entire world, but the problem is that it will not provide it to those who cannot pay. How can that be good? Can you remember from the Bible when the 5000 were fed? That was not a miracle. It was just common sense. Some in the crowd had nothing to eat, while others had more than they needed. The simple solution was for the haves to share with the have-nots. The miracle was that those with more shared with those who had nothing."

"You are inheritors of a system that works efficiently to produce great wealth, but it fails to distribute that wealth fairly. It neglects the poor and those in the middle so those at the top can accrue more than is justly needed." Jesus raised his hands toward the sky as he continued, "this is evil of the vilest form. If you do not fight against this evil, then you become a part of the evil."

178

Someone in the crowd shouted, "but the government will send out thugs to subdue us."

Jesus, unperturbed, replied, "if you are not marred by scars, by sweat, blood and tears, then you have not been in the fight. If you are not valiant, what can be gained? You can come up short time and time again because effort produces errors and shortcomings. Yet, if you fail, you fail while daring to confront injustice. He who fears the taste of defeat shall never know victory."

Jesus sighted a man in a wheelchair, obviously a quadriplegic, and pointed at him. "This man is paralyzed from the neck down. Too many of us walk around and are paralyzed from the neck up. If you fear failure you will never experience success. There was an American man who was considered grotesque to gaze upon. Yet, that did not keep him from seeking political office. He failed in business at 31. He was defeated for the state legislature at 32. He failed in business again at 34. He had a nervous breakdown at 36. He was defeated for election to various elective offices at 38, 43, 46, 48, 55, 56 and 58. At 60, Abraham Lincoln was elected President of this country. He realized that failure was not the end. Failure can be used as a stepping stone to success by the wise and prudent."

179

Jesus looked out at the crowd and said, "I shall not be returning to the park again. I hope that I have sowed seeds that you will plant, so mighty trees with many branches will sprout from what you have learned here."

A tall, thin, elderly woman at the front of the crowd almost screaming said, "please, don't leave us. We have become dependent on you for guidance."

Jesus smiled at the woman and began a parable. "It is the custom of many Native Americans to take their teenage sons into the wilderness as part of the rights of passage. A father once took his son into the wilderness in the middle of the night. The boy was required to sit alone on a stump blindfolded all night and not remove it until he felt the sun's rays on his face. At that time, he could find his way back to his father who would be waiting in the village. The boy agreed to do as told, but sitting there with the blindfold on, he was terrified as he heard the sounds of wild beasts all about him. The howling wind nearly blew him off the stump, but still he sat as instructed. Finally, after feeling the rays of the sun, he removed his blindfold, and there was his father on the stump, sitting next to him. He had stood watch all night to protect him. So, like that father, I promise to be

180

with you always. Just look in your heart where my strength now resides."

Jesus stepped down from the table, walked past Mary, Dixon and Matthew with his outstretched hands, motioning for them to follow him. As they exited the park, the three ministers, some of their congregation members and a local politician were waiting for them. The politician came up and said, "at the behest of my constituents here, I would like to speak to you. I am Congressman Biddle."

Jesus, seemingly not particularly interested, replied, "we can talk I suppose. What did you want to talk about?"

The Congressman, a man of about 50 with a pencil thin moustache and an erect bearing that smacked of arrogance replied, "well, I think we should talk about how you are riling people up and becoming a public nuisance."

Jesus, calmly replied, "my time is very valuable, because I have so little of it. Before we talk, could I ask you a question?"

The Congressman, somewhat taken aback by the boldness of this man, replied, "sure, ask away."

As the Son of Thunder

Mary, Dixon and Matthew all knew what was coming, but the Congressman was unaware that he had fallen into a trap. Jesus said, "O.K., a horse, a cow and a deer all eat the same stuff – grass. Yet a dear excretes little pellets, while a cow turns out a flat patty and a horse produces clumps. Why do you suppose in the great scheme of things this occurs?"

Mystified the Congressman replied, "how the hell do I know?'

Jesus smiled and said, "you want to have a discussion with me? Why should I waste my time, you don't know shit."

Jesus and his three friends walked away laughing, while the ministers, the congregation members and the Congressman all stood there with confused looks on their faces, dumbfounded by the refusal of this man to respect authority.

Jesus looked at Dixon and said, "I told you I was a one man revolution."

All four enjoyed another good laugh as they proceeded up the street, heading downtown. Just as they neared Main Street, there was that familiar black sedan, moving ever so slowly behind them.

182

As the Son of Thunder

The three friends all seemed concerned about being followed. Jesus stopped and said, "I know their kind from many times in the past. These are the people who poisoned Socrates, burned Joan of Arc, hanged, tortured and dismembered countless others during the Inquisition. Time after time, the forces of darkness try to extinguish the light of knowledge. These are people who think they serve God and country, but they only serve the forces of eternal darkness. I have integrity on my side, so all things are possible. They think they have God on their side, so all things are permissible. I shall suffer as I have suffered before, but my suffering pales in comparison to the suffering these people bring to their souls. I assure you that I shall be absolved in the book of life. They shall be condemned, and the light of their souls will be extinguished even as they walk about. They are nothing but dead men walking."

Matthew, looking perplexed and worried, as he looked back at the car that was creeping along the street behind them, said, "but the devil is at work among us, and you seem unconcerned."

Jesus replied, "the devil is an invention of those who use fear to control the minds of people unable to think for themselves. The evil in this world is put here by men, not by the devil"

183

Mary, touching Jesus softly on the arm, pensively asked, "but do you not have the power to alter events that might lead to your demise?"

Jesus smiled and said, "I don't alter events, I encourage others to alter them. We all have great power, if we would only use it in concert with one another. Death is inevitable, but life isn't. Most people fear life more than they fear death. They just don't realize it."

An elderly woman came up and touched Jesus' arm. In a gravely, barely audible voice she said, "I have heard you for days now, and I just want to know if you are he whom I have worshipped for so many years, and longed to see return to bring peace to the world.

Jesus reached down, placed his hand on her frail shoulder and said, "I do not bring peace. I bring a sword to cut a swath through the hearts of those who embrace injustice. The power of the exalted cedes nothing to those who cry for justice. I say to the wealthy and powerful that as long as there is no justice there will be no peace. The poor and the enslaved should wait not for a saviour, because they can be their own saviours. Stop waiting for God to act. Even at your age, you still have a mind, use that mind to save yourself and others."

As the Son of Thunder

Perplexed the woman said, "are you not the one who walked on water?"

Almost laughing Jesus said, "my dear woman, do you genuinely believe a man could walk on water? Are you not too old for fairy tales? If one walks on a sandbar at high tide, it can appear that one is walking on water. Every thing in your Bible can be plausibly explained if you open up your mind, rather than turn it over to the purveyors of deceit. Put aside silliness and embrace the reality that each person is a God. We all are capable of performing miracles, the miracles of love, justice for our fellow man, a fair distribution of wealth, compassion and understanding."

As usual, a crowd began to gather around Jesus. Looking to the rear, Dixon saw the black sedan had pulled to the curb, and the black SUV had pulled in behind it. What were they up to now? Why did Jesus seem so unconcerned about their intentions?

A rotund man of about fifty asked Jesus if everyone who did not accept Christ was doomed. Jesus calmly replied, "what kind of God would doom a child to hell for not knowing he existed? Anyone who worshipped that cruel a God is himself practicing cruelty of the vilest form."

As the Son of Thunder

A strikingly beautiful woman asked Jesus what she could do to serve him. His reply was simple and direct. "You are not here to serve me. I am here to serve you. My words serve your interests and will explain to you how to stop being a slave to your oppressors."

Across the street was a magnificently ornate church with a golden cross atop its soaring spire. As the sun glistened off the spire and the rays bounced about, an effeminate young man pointed to it and said, "that is where I was told that I need to seek salvation. As a small child, I attended that church, and the teachers there told me that I am doomed, because I am sexually attracted to men. Am I really doomed? Is there any way I can overcome this evil that makes me want to lie in the embrace of another man?"

"My son, the evil is not in you. The evil is in those who condemn you. Your sexuality has nothing to do with goodness. Throughout history, churches have been dens of inequity where fear is used to ridicule, belittle and condemn. Be proud of what is in your heart. If you love another man, walk down the street hand-in-hand with him and your head held high in complete defiance of those who condemn love. What kind of God would find any love between two human beings abhorrent?"

186

Pointing to the spire, Jesus continued. "What is detestable is not the love between two people of the same sex. It is the construction of magnificent edifices to intolerance while allowing poverty, famine and injustice to exist. If the church was doing its job, those evils would not exist, because its leaders would demand justice for those mired poverty."

Another man piped in, "so, you don't believe we should be awed by the sign of the cross?"

Jesus, with a mischievous smile slowly pursing across his lips, replied, "if you had been crucified, do you think you would appreciate seeing so many crosses when your returned?"

The crowd roared with laughter, and Jesus continued. "if we were to walk over to that church now, it would be locked, just as you lock the doors to your homes. Why would an institution supposedly dedicated to serving man lock its doors? Do they fear a homeless person caught in a raging storm might seek shelter? Do they fear that a person who needs a place to sleep at night might lie down on a pew? Do they fear that someone who needs sustenance might steal the bread and wine used for communion? Did the son of man not say those who are blessed with wealth should

187

give all they have to the poor? Well, isn't the church rich? Why do they not put into practice what they preach? What kind of God would want magnificent edifices erected to his glory while the very people he is supposed to love wallow in poverty?"

As always, the crowd was awed by this mysterious man. His final words as he walked away were, "and now I go to meet my fate. Remember me, but more important, remember my words and take the action needed to save yourselves and your loved ones from the evil that is all about you in the form of poverty, ignorance and dedication to an economic system based on greed."

Exhausted from telling Aaron about Jesus, Mary sighed and a tear dropped delicately down her right cheek. Wiping it away, she said, "there was a finality to the way he walked home with us, almost as if he knew it would be his last night with us. I can't explain it, but there was a heaviness in his manner that I had never seen before."

Aaron, not in any way convinced of the divinity of this man, but still intrigued by all he had heard said, "tell me what occurred when you got home."

188

As the Son of Thunder

"Well, it was a bit unusual, as Matthew and Jesus seemed to be particularly apprehensive, as if they were waiting for something to occur. Dixon and I were watching television when Matthew looked out the window and said to Jesus that it is time."

Mary, with a pensive look continued, "they got up, said their goodbyes and the last thing Jesus said haunts me."

Rubbing his hands together between his parted legs. Aaron said, "and what did he say?"

"Well, I suppose it wasn't just the what he said, but the way he said it. For the first time I sensed apprehension in his voice and consternation on his face. He just said that we should remember that all religions are based on myths. That we should never fear death, and never be a slave to religion where fear of death is used to keep us from really living. He said that people need a saviour, because they are too fearful to save themselves from the evils of a world based on self-interest and unmitigated greed, and that there have been thousands of religions over the years with virgin born saviours who were supposed to solve the problems we should solve for ourselves. Until we learned to save ourselves, there was no hope."

189

Aaron, not convinced of any divinity on the part of Jesus, but still immensely impressed by all he had heard, sit mystified as he gazed at the lovely Mary. "And that was it, he just left."

"He left with Matthew, who was also pensive and walked out with his head bowed. At the door, Matthew turned and said that he would return by midnight."

"Dixon and I waited patiently for his return, but by 2:00AM, we were worried when neither of them had showed up. I left the door unlocked in case Matthew returned, and Dixon and I decided to walk downtown to see if we could find them. About two blocks from the apartment building, a beaten and bloodied Matthew was stumbling down the street. He fell into Dixon's arms and just said that it was done and that evil had triumphed. Matthew reached into his pocket, pulling out a tattered, empty cigarette pack and handed it to Dixon. He died in Dixon's arms without uttering another word."

Aaron scratched his forehead and said, "I have seen the cigarette pack, and it just had a brief message from Jesus about remembering him. I assume you reported Matthew's death to the sheriff?"

As the Son of Thunder

"We did, but all he said was that it was probably one vagrant killing another vagrant for pocket change or for drugs. The next day, when I filed a report about Jesus' disappearance, he intonated that maybe Jesus could have killed Matthew or just skipped town like most vagrants do when they run out of soft touches in a community. I don't think he ever intended to search for Jesus. He just filed the report, because he didn't want any more trouble from me."

Aaron got up, extended his hand as a signal for Mary to rise. She stoically stood before Aaron, grasping his hand. Both smiling, they headed for the bedroom. Aaron whispered softly, "I want to hold you, caress you and feel your warmth. I know this man has touched you deeply, and although I have never met him, your recounting of the goodness in him makes me long to be in his presence, not to accept him as a deity, but to bask in the glow of one who sees the evil that is afoot in this country and all across the globe from the terror perpetrated by the corporate and religious theocracy. I promise you that tomorrow we shall initiate the search for him. Dead or alive, I will find him, and for those who might have harmed him, I shall bring, not the wrath of any fairy-tale God, but the wrath of Aaron Adams.

191

CHAPTER 12
IN SEARCH OF THE LIGHT

In the presence of Mary, Aaron felt alive. Yet, it was autumn in New Jersey, and autumn there was a time for dying. The browning leaves were clinging to life, but they hung precariously on the trees, waiting for the inevitable fall to the ground where they would be trampled, raked, burned or decompose into the soil.

As they walked the streets, heading for the sheriff's office, Aaron instinctively read the faces of the people as they passed. Most of them had that dull recognition and listless hang to their heads. Summer was dying and the decay was all about. It seemed that only Aaron and Mary were truly alive among the dead people walking, as they, although concerned about Jesus, had a smile on their faces and a bounce to their step. Love did that to people.

Aaron gazed upon Mary and thought of the moist kisses from her succulent lips. Her dark hair, blowing gently back from her face, framed it perfectly, and she was not just smiling with her lips, her eyes danced with glee, too. Watching her breasts bounce provocatively, reminded Aaron of the carnal instincts she had resurrected in him.

192

The languid people continued heading to mundane jobs that had made slaves of them, so they could pay mortgages on elaborate homes they didn't need, buy cars that were more status symbols than transportation and to accumulate all the toys that they thought were necessary for the good life. These were the very people who Jesus had tried to save, but they were too conditioned by the powerful forces that brainwashed them every day to see that they were lining up to be made slaves.

Walking into the sheriff's office, they were met by a female clerk who seemed determined to make certain that the public, which she was supposed to serve, was treated with complete disdain. Not even looking up from the newspaper, she said, "what you want?"

Aaron, forever the malcontent who refused to bow before arrogance, replied, "I want some courtesy and a little service for the public you are here to serve. I need to see Sheriff Dillon."

Taken aback by Aaron's direct manner, the strikingly beautiful woman, who was probably hired for her looks rather than her skill, looked up from her newspaper and replied, "unless it's an emergency, you will need to make an appointment

193

to see the sheriff."

"Then, it's an emergency," bellowed Aaron.

The clerk, now getting a bit perturbed said, "and, what is the emergency," as she slowly rose and stuck out her chest that was securely wrapped in a bullet proof vest that fought a losing battle in confining the magnificent orbs that pushed against it.

"The emergency is a man who has been missing for some time and the apparent lack of concern from this department to investigate his disappearance."

As Aaron was letting his displeasure be known, Sheriff Dillon walked out of his office and curtly said, "what the hell are you two doing here? I told you this con-man you are so keen to find just skipped town, like all bums eventually do when they find out the people of Woodbury Creek aren't such easy pickings. He was just trying to stir up envy among the poor."

Aaron, now warming up to the verbal sparring was set to let loose with both barrels. "You sound like a Christian, justifying poverty by quoting Jesus who said the poor we have always."

194

As the Son of Thunder

Aaron stiffened his back and stared directly at the sheriff. "Well, I ain't no Christian, and I have complete disdain for arrogant assholes who can justify any abrogation of social justice with a Bible. You call a guy a bum, because he is down on his luck or doesn't have the mental capacity to earn a living. The real bums are the assholes like you who live off the public dole and decry minimal welfare for those not lucky enough to get a cushiony job or be born into wealth. You are not dealing with the typical citizen who will accept your arrogance and cower in fear. I am Aaron Adams, and I am going to get to the bottom of this affair."

Not accustomed to being talked to that way, the sheriff stood in silence for a second. He looked at the clerk, who now had placed her hand on the gun in her holster, and he made a slight motion left to right with his head indicating she should not un-holster her gun.

The sheriff licked his lower lip and said, "look Adams, you are treading on thin ice here. There is no need to get on your high horse."

Without hesitation, Aaron replied, "I am on a high horse, because I am tired of being jerked around. I need some answers."

195

"Look Adams, I already told Miss Madison, I would do all I can. I sent out an alert, but no one has responded. I'm not going out looking for a bum we are all glad to be rid of. All he did was cause trouble while he was here. Now, he has moved onto some other town, where he is causing some other sheriff problems."

Aaron, placing his hand on the counter, leaned slightly forward and said, "you put out an alert. What does that prove? You know more than you are telling. What about the F.B.I. and the National Security Agency being here. I know you were seen talking with the F.B.I. and the N.S.A. This country is filled with government goons rounding up anybody who dares speak out against injustice and oppression. Why don't you check with them to see if they know anything, or are you part of a cover-up promulgated by the fascists running this nation now?"

The sheriff was becoming indignant. "Listen, you son-of-bitch. You don't come in my office and accuse me of a cover-up. I'm the law around here, and regardless of what you think of me, I deserve some respect. This country is filled with assholes like you always ready to accuse the government of malfeasance, when all we are doing is protecting you."

196

Now, Aaron was really perturbed. "Sheriff, you sound like a graduate of the fucking Dick Cheney School of Torture. I suppose you think water boarding is just an enhanced interrogation technique when used by the USA, but is torture when used by another country. I have been dealing with sunshine patriots like you ever since I hit the jungles of Vietnam. You are the kind of person who can drop bombs on women and children from 80,000 feet and not call it terrorism. I have had a belly full of you assholes who think using terrorism to fight terrorism is justifiable as long as this country is doing it. People like you would have been at home in WW II Germany forcing the Jews into cattle cars. You think patriotism is supporting your country right or wrong. The true patriot questions his country and refuses to bow before its tyranny."

The Sheriff headed toward his office. As he got to the door, he turned slightly and said, "get the fuck out of here. I have said all I am saying to you. I am warning you – back off."

Aaron smiled and replied, "well, I am not intimidated by you, sheriff. I will get out, but just remember that I am like a pit pull. I have my teeth in this case, and I won't let it go until it is solved, regardless of who tells me to back off."

197

Motioning to the silent Mary to follow him, the two of them headed out the door. As they turned to the right outside, they peered into the sheriff's office window. He was frantically talking on the phone and making gestures with his hands. Who was he calling, and what was he saying? Aaron knew it had something to do with what just occurred in the sheriff's office.

As they rounded the corner, Aaron glanced to his left and noticed a black sedan moving slowly up the street behind them. Placing his hand on Mary's arms he whispered, "don't be obvious, but take a look behind us. Have you every seen that car before?"

Discreetly looking behind her, Mary replied, "I have seen it many times. The last time was when it followed me, Dixon, Matthew and Jesus to my apartment."

Gently pushing Mary against a building, Aaron said, "stay here," as he turned quickly and walked straight toward the car. Stepping off the curb, into the street before the car could speed up, he was actually blocking it. Looking at the white-haired man driving, he leaned on the hood and said, "you F.B.I. or N.S.A.," just as the people in traffic behind them started blowing their horns.

198

The white haired man replied, "listen jerk, I am Agent Shaw with the F.B.I. Get your goddamn hands off the car and step back onto the sidewalk."

Aaron defiantly replied, as he motioned for the cars honking horns to go around, "run over me asshole, or get out of the car and tell me why I am being followed."

The agent on the passenger side got out and pointed for Aaron to move to the sidewalk as he pulled his gun. Aaron, figuring discretion was the better part of valour, did as asked.

Agent Shaw pulled the car to the curb, got out and went over to Aaron, who was standing beside the other agent. Standing toe-to-toe with Aaron, he said, "not that it is any of your business, but we received a notice from our New York office to keep an eye on you. You are suspected of possibly aiding and abating terrorism."

Aaron said, in a mocking manner, "aiding terrorism? Every time this nation bombs another country, when our government shoves its brand of corporate slavery on another nation or it overthrows governments it doesn't like, the USA is engaging in terrorism of the vilest form, but you assholes are worried about me being a terrorist?"

199

Aaron got so close to Agent Shaw that he could hear his breathing. "I am here to find out about another possible victim of American terrorism, maybe carried out by you guys."

Slightly glancing to his left at the agent holding the gun, Aaron continued, "this asshole with the gun thinks I am afraid of him, but if I wanted, I could kill both of you right now where you stand and it would happen so fast, neither one of you would see it coming."

The agent with the gun sucked in some air and stood more erect, his gun shaking slightly in his hand as Aaron continued, "hey, don't get nervous tough guy. I said I could kill you. I didn't say I would."

Agent Shaw, now becoming more angered, said, "Adams, it is a crime to threaten a federal officer."

Aaron, obviously unperturbed, replied, "yeah, and in a democratic country, it should be illegal for a federal officer to threaten a citizen. I am just walking down the street, and my government thinks it has the right to tail me, because I might be a danger, not because I am a danger. You guys think you are protecting democracy, but you are all a pack of fascist bastards."

As the Son of Thunder

Looking directly into Agent Shaw's eyes, Aaron said, "tell that asshole to put his gun away. If you don't, both of you will not live to regret it. You think you have the drop on me, but believe me, I have the drop on you. You just don't know it. The same government that trained you to trample all over citizen's rights, also trained me to be an assassin, and believe me, I was good at my job."

Agent Shaw looked to his right and said, "put it away."

Reluctantly, the agent put away his gun and Aaron, smiling with glee, said, "O.K., now let's talk about what you guys may have done with this man Jesus. I just want to know if he is safe and what you might have charged him with."

Agent Shaw, seemingly more relaxed now, was not about to admit that the government had Jesus. However, he did offer a hypothetical response. "Suppose someone in the government did apprehend this man? Why wouldn't the news media know about it? After all, he would be considered a threat to national security, and the media would be all over that. I am not saying he was apprehended. I am just saying I could see the justification for it, as inciting people to commit acts of rebellion is dangerous."

201

Aaron, sensing a real opening, replied, "yeah, that kind of thinking would have kept the colonists from rebelling against England. Urging people to throw off the yoke of oppression is a real threat to those who have all the weapons and all the power. You might have to waste some bullets and bombs on people rebelling against the tyranny of the wealthy and powerful."

Up the street, Mary was growing more tense as she watched Aaron sparring with the two agents. However, she was determined to do as Aaron said, so she patiently stood there against the wall.

Agent Shaw motioned for the other agent to get into the car, and he, himself, started walking away. He turned to Aaron and said, "the best thing you can do is get out-of-town, Adams. Keep your nose out of what is going on down here, there are enough problems in New York to keep you busy."

As Aaron turned to head back up the street, he noticed an older grey haired lady in the back of the car. For an instance, she looked familiar to him, but he was distracted when Agent Shaw said, "I see you again, and I promise you it won't be pleasant. You are a menace, and we know how to deal with people who threaten peace and tranquility. Watch your step."

202

Aaron, without hesitation, said, as Agent Shaw opened the car door, "and you watch yours."

The tête-à-tête over, Aaron walked back up to Mary. Smiling, he took her by the arm, and they continued their walk up the street. Aaron asked if any local ministers had voiced support for Jesus. Saying she wasn't sure, but that she knew that three ministers in town had tried to meet with him for days, but Jesus had avoided them, as he said that the church was nothing more than a tax-dodging corporation run for the benefit of the few at the expense of the many who were foolish enough to toss money into a collection plate.

Aaron, smiled broadly and said, "sounds like he had a pretty good handle on what the church is all about."

Mary replied, "well, he never seemed too impressed with the church. He always said that a church kept people in bondage to ignorance by hiding the truth, and that he was here to offer the truth to those willing to listen."

Aaron asked Mary if she knew where he could find any of the three ministers. Looking to her right, Mary pointed at the huge church across the street and said, "right there, Reverend Townsend."

203

As the Son of Thunder

The huge grey opulent edifice, probably built in the early 1980's, towered into the sky. Fluffy white clouds moved slowly behind the two steeples that were topped with cooper domes. The church totally dominated the downtown area. Its opulence stood out even more as it was surrounded by boarded up buildings and a few modest homes nearby. Walking across the street, Aaron and Mary squinted their eyes to word off the intensity of the glare coming off the enormous four cooper-covered doors. Walking up the magnificent Italian marble steps to the doors, Aaron was not at all surprised when he found them locked. After all, why would a church be open to those who might want to pray? The lonely souls wandering the streets were not to be saved, but to be feared. They might damage the church if allowed in to worship a God who obviously was too busy looking out for the rich and powerful to be bothered by those trapped in economic slavery to the moneyed class. Aaron remembered times, when as a youth, he would freely go into churches, as they were open 24 hours a day to offer solace to the sick and weary. But now, a society based on greed had created so much poverty that the very people the church was supposed to help were shunted aside and looked on as parasites seeking a handout from just another corporate entity that hid behind the cross and a promise of pie in the sky.

Walking to the side of the church, there was a white gate with a sign indicating where the office was located. Aaron pushed the flawlessly whitewashed gate open and proceeded with Mary down an elaborate stone walkway that was surrounded by an immaculately manicured lawn. The magnificent fountains spraying water in steady streams made Aaron smile, as he thought of his own fountain of man batter that had sprayed forth into Mary the night before. Yeah, Aaron was really proud of his performance, and he couldn't wait to perform again.

At the end of the walkway was a gold plated door. It, too, was locked. Overhead was a video camera, and to the right of the door a buzzer that indicated you needed to ring for admission. Shaking his head at the elaborate security needed to protect a house of God, Aaron looked at Mary and said, "you think this place would even let a scraggily-glad, long haired Jesus in to pray?"

Laughingly, Mary replied, "not unless he had a big bundle of cash with him."

A buzzer sounded and a voice said, "could we help you?"

"Aaron Adams to see Reverend Townsend."

205

"Do you have an appointment?"

"No, but it is urgent that I talk with him."

Rather curtly, the female voice replied, "just a minute."

Waiting impatiently, Aaron frowned and looked about the gloriously maintained garden. The curtness of the woman continued. "The Reverend doesn't know you, and you are not on the congregation rolls. Could you state your specific business."

Aaron, now, reaching the end of his patience replied, "listen lady, is this a church or a goddamn prison. I could get into the White House easier than I can get into this place. I need to see the reverend to discuss a matter of utmost importance to the church. Am I going to see him, or do I have to interrupt church service on Sunday by walking up to him while he is delivering his sermon?"

Suddenly a deep, resonant, arrogant-toned voice interrupted and said, "I generally require an appointment to meet with non-members, but I can spare a few minutes. I will buzz you in, but please be brief, as I have a luncheon with the local Rotary Club in about 30 minutes."

As the Son of Thunder

How does one accurately describe a place that is supposed to be dedicated to serving mankind? The vestibule was opulently decorated with a wainscot made of deep, dark walnut that rose about three feet to a chair rail that was gold-trimmed. Above the rail was a velvet wallpaper with silver lining up to the walnut crown moulding that blended with the coffered ceiling that had golden sprinkles that gave the illusions of twinkling stars. Walking through the walnut encrusted archway, one entered into a huge sitting room with Louis the 15th sofas and chairs, all trimmed in gold. Sitting behind an oblong glass desk was an immaculately attired blond of about 30 with huge breasts that seemed to be fighting for freedom from the expensive blouse that imprisoned them. A scowl crossed her lips as she pointed to a walnut door that had an ornate golden plate in the middle that read *The Reverend Dr. Townsend*. "You may go in. Dr. Townsend is waiting for you."

The door was so heavy that Aaron felt a strain in his wrist as he pushed it open. The opulence Aaron and Mary had seen before paled with what their eyes feasted on in the Reverend's office. The grandiose nature of the room was almost overwhelming. Their feet were on a fine Persian rug with magnificently woven battle scenes. Overhead were incredibly ornate frescoes depicting angels, God, Jesus and various scenes from the Bible. The walls were dark walnut trimmed in Italian marble with niches carved into them where backlit vases and statues set gloriously among the splendorous office that was a big as a small home.

Sitting behind a huge kidney shaped white desk with inlaid leather was a well-dressed man of about 40. His yellow silk tie was knotted perfectly and he reached up with his left hand, placed his thumb under the tie, and gently slid his hand down to straightened it, while he leaned back arrogantly in his overstuffed Corinthian leather chair.

Not a single strand was out of place on his immaculately combed thick black hair. Strikingly handsome, his skin was deeply tanned, as if he had just spent the day basking in the sun. Not bothering to get up or shake hands, he simply pointed at the magnificent Edwardian settee in front of the desk, his splendidly manicured nails glistening in the light projected by the antique desk lamp.

Aaron and Mary sit down and before they got comfortable, the Reverend Townsend blurted out, "I don't know you Mr. Adams, but I know Ms. Madison by reputation. I do not make it a habit of

208

of spending my valuable time with known prostitutes."

Passing up the opportunity to give the Reverend a piece of his mind, Aaron simply placed his hand on Mary's leg and replied, "I don't have time to discuss Mary's occupation with you. I am here to find out what you know about the disappearance of the man who was calling himself Jesus."

The reverend took a deep breath and leaned slightly forward. "First, call him by his right name. It should be Heh-soos, not Jesus. It is a sacrilege to call that man by the name of our lord and saviour. He was nothing more than an anarchist masquerading as a man of God.."

Aaron, realizing that he needed to glean information from the Reverend Townsend, was careful not to antagonize him with any verbal retorts before getting what he required. However, he was making mental notes of things he would use in the inevitable torrent of indignation he would pour out once he had what he needed from the pompous, self-righteous, arrogant son-of-bitch.

Aaron, fighting back his resentment of this monument to intolerance, calmly asked when did the reverend last see Jesus.

209

Townsend got a quizzical look on his face and said, "well, he agreed to meet me right here at the church the night he apparently disappeared. I was in the sanctuary when he came in with that vagabond friend of his called Matthew. I, and several of my ministerial colleagues, had decided that I should discuss his activities in Woodbury Creek with him and maybe offer him some cash to leave town and stop antagonizing so many people. I did so. He took nearly two hundred dollars that I handed him, and said he would put it to good use, but that no Judas was going to force him to stop telling the truth. The truth, what a laugh. He wouldn't know the truth if it slapped him in the face. We are out two hundred dollars, but it was money well spent to rid this community of his vile attempts to sew disharmony among the populace."

Aaron glanced up at the crystal chandelier with its sweeping arms spreading outward from its core that presided over the opulent office from twenty feet above. He tried valiantly to hide his disdain for this arrogant ass who literally infected the air about him and diffused an insidious evil that made a mockery of all he was supposed to represent. The room itself seemed to be filled with a melancholic anguish that permeated into its deepest corners. Aaron abruptly rose from the settee, took Mary by the hand and pulled her up.

210

As the Son of Thunder

Looking directly in Reverend Townsend's eyes, Aaron's contempt boiled to the surface in a tirade that made this so-called servant of God think that the gates of hell were opening and he was about to be swallowed up in the eternal fires of damnation.

Still holding Mary's hand, Aaron said, "first you arrogant, self-centered son-of-bitch, you insulted my friend here. For that I should shove my fist so far down your throat that I could tickle your tonsils. You have the nerve to judge her when you prostitute yourself every day in this monument to greed and intolerance you call a church by selling a pack of mindless, docile, apathetic sheep a bunch of fairy tales that any smart five year old would laugh at. You preach about compassion and love, then lock your doors to keep the homeless from sleeping on your unused pews. You talk about love for your fellow man while supporting wars and allowing the gross inequity perpetrated by an unjust economic system. You dine on caviar while all about you are those who beg for scraps from the table of plenty. You rant and rave against unjustness and sit idly by as your government tortures, incarcerates or kills all who dare oppose it. If I believed in God, I would rather rot in hell than have to spend eternity with assholes like you. A pitchfork up my ass would be a small price to pay in order to be free of tyrannical, self-serving

211

hypocrites like you."

Having heard all he could take without a response, Reverend Townsend got up, but before he could utter a word, Aaron said, "don't open your mouth, asshole. I am walking out of this den of evil to breath some fresh air and mingle with those for whom you have nothing but disdain. One day the holes in the bellies of those you repress with economic inequity will grow so large that they will put guns in their hands. Then, they will exercise the 2nd Amendment rights you so greedily protect to blow the brains out of you blood-sucking, greedy, hypocritical bastards."

Turning quickly and tugging on Mary's hand, Aaron looked at her and smiled. She smiled back as the dumfounded reverend eased back into his chair. He immediately reached for his phone as Aaron and Mary heard the receiver being picked up and the frantic pushing of buttons to dial a number.

Aaron and Mary walked out of the darkness in search of the light.

CHAPTER 13
OMINOUS SIGN OF COMING TURMOIL

Aaron wondered who these people were calling every time he walked out of their presence. Obviously there was some conspiratorial chicanery involved. All of them were aware of something that was being hidden. Something that they did not want to share with Aaron and Mary.

Seemingly out of leads, Aaron asked Mary if there was anyone else who might have any knowledge of what occurred that last night when Jesus disappeared. Mary could not think of anyone, but then Aaron said, "are there any street people who hang out downtown? Any people who might frequent alleys and little niches that are secluded?"

Realizing that there were, like in so many other American towns, those who were forced to live on the margins of society, Mary replied, "sure, sure, I should have thought of that. There are many people living on the streets. One is named Simon, and he knows everyone of the derelicts who scrounge about for food and beg for a few cents. If anyone saw anything, Simon would know about it, because he is sort of the crown prince of the poor around here. Everyone knows him."

213

Although it was autumn, this was a sizzling hot day in New Jersey. As the two seekers of truth pondered about in the alley ways of Woodbury Creek in search of the man called Simon, the stench of human excrement, disposed garbage and people who had no place to bathe penetrated more than their nostrils. It reached deep within their souls. How could a country that professed itself a Christian nation allow this kind of poverty and neglect to exist while those at the top of the economic ladder lived in splendorous luxury?

Aaron thought to himself that poverty was the parent of crime. Unfortunately, it was not the parent of revolution in a country where the poor were so complacent and accepting of their fate that they refused to band together and demand justice. Rather than preying on the garbage bins in search of a few scraps of food, the homeless should arm themselves and march on the gated estates of the rich to demand their share from the table of plenty.

Looking at many of these poor souls who were obviously laid waste by drugs, Aaron thought about how many people who pointed the finger of condemnation at these so-called miscreants were lining up at pharmacies to get their legally dispensed drugs from the corporate pushers who were licensed and approved by the government.

214

Walking down a dark, dingy alley that was surrounded on three sides by eight story buildings, just as they were about to call it a day, Mary pointed at an emaciated man dressed in tattered overalls seated against the wall. He was so darkly tanned that it appeared his skin had literally soaked up the heat of the day. His eyes were as black as coal, wide, pleading, begging for mercy where there was none. He was no longer a man, just a part of the litter that cluttered the alley. He was sweating profusely. You could see that his body ached, but his soul was already dead. He was just one of the many who had been forgotten by a society where poverty was not a social condition. It was a disease that others feared was contagious; therefore, those with the disease were supposed to be shunned like the lepers of long ago. Pointing at the shell of a man, Mary simply uttered, "it is Simon."

Simon, managing a smile upon recognizing Mary, said, "my goodness, how are you Mary?"

Aaron picked up a nearby crate and placed it in front of Simon for Mary to sit on. Mary, reached out, touched Simon on the shoulder and said, "I am fine Simon. This is my friend Aaron Adams, and he is investigating the disappearance of Jesus. Would you talk with him?"

215

Somewhat surprised by Aaron's willingness to shake his dirty hand, Simon obviously appreciated the gesture, saying, "a real pleasure, Mr. Adams."

"Pleasure to meet you, too. We are trying to trace the whereabouts of this man on the night he apparently disappeared. Do you recall seeing anything unusual at any time, as Mary says you usually know what is going on downtown."

Simon cleared his throat and said, "well, you have to be careful around here just how much you see, as it can get you in trouble. I see a lot of things that I quickly forget in order to not anger the wrong people. Talking to you is probably not good for my well-being, if you know what I mean."

Aaron replied, "I can understand that, and I promise you that whatever you tell us will be kept in the strictest confidence. No one will ever know we ever got any information from you."

Simon looked at Mary with his dark eyes, almost pleading for her assistance. Mary smiled and said, "you can trust Aaron. You have my solemn word, Simon."

Nodding his head, Simon replied, "O.K."

As the Son of Thunder

Seemingly assured that he could trust these two people, Simon began to disclose what he knew of the final night Jesus roamed the streets of Woodbury Creek. His reluctance was obvious, but his faith and trust in Mary was a catalyst that made him willing to take the risk. He started with an intelligent philosophical review of what this man had meant to him and the others forced to a life of begging for sustenance in a land of plenty.

"First, we were all surprised when this mysterious man joined us night after night, sharing our meagre amount of food and makeshift beds in this alley of despair. We sensed that it was not necessary for him to be here, but that he simply chose to be among what he called the real people in a land of false promise. To say he was a radical is an understatement. He told us of how the conservatives of his time had crucified him, because he dared to appeal to the free, the restless and the progressive people who longed to throw off the chains of oppression. He said that the modern church was an abomination in his eyes, because its sacraments, its hierarchy and especially its claim to infallibility were all counter to everything he stood for. He said that religion had been corrupted, because man did not need to worship, did not need a hierarchy, did not need to tithe nor did he need to suffer."

217

Aaron was growing impatient, as he wanted to get to the night of Jesus' disappearance, but he was too kind to interrupt this man who was enjoying the interest and respect these two from the outside world were showing him.

Continuing, Simon's eyes seemed to dance with glee at the willingness of these two to listen intently to his story. "So, for several nights, he shared our little alley world. Then, he said that he was going to venture forth and share his words with others who were seeking the truth. We went to the park many times to hear him, and mingled there with Mary, Dixon, Matthew and others who found comfort and inspiration in his words. He often returned here to sit and talk with us, to share food and to bring us comfort."

Realizing that these two were anxiously awaiting to hear what he knew about the disappearance, Simon said, "O.K., O.K., so now I will get to the night of his disappearance. I was at the entrance to the alley when I saw him walking down the other side of Main Street. As he turned to go into the church, he caught a glimpse of me in the alley and waved. I acknowledged him. He went up the steps into the church. When the doors closed, they made a hollow sound, and I thought to myself that it was a sinister sign."

218

"Soon, Jesus' friend, Matthew showed up and went into the church, too. Almost immediately, upon the closing of the doors behind Matthew, two ministers I know walked up with Sheriff Dillon. They stood on the steps and a black sedan followed by a black SUV pulled up in front of the church. Seven men and a woman got out of the vehicles. They stood there talking to the sheriff and the two ministers. The sheriff and the ministers walked down the street about 500 feet. The others got back in the vehicles and drove down the street to join them. A white haired man pointed at the church and then the seven men, one woman and the sheriff located themselves in various places along the street. The ministers apparently left and I ducked a little farther into the alley in hopes that I would not be noticed."

Mary and Aaron seemed entranced by Simon's tale. He continued. "Jesus and Matthew came out of the church. They both immediately headed for the alley entrance. As they walked into the alley, I frantically told Jesus that there were some people apparently getting ready to ambush him. He smiled, handed me $200, telling me to share it with the others, and said something about he was always destined to meet his fate, because the church leaders were the modern day Judases who had betrayed him once again."

As the Son of Thunder

"I peaked around the corner as he and Matthew walked down the street in the direction of those men who were apparently waiting for them. What followed has preyed on my mind ever since, but I have been too afraid to tell anyone what I saw for fear of retribution. I am like Simon Peter from the Bible, I have denied knowing the man many times to others for fear of what might befall me. I am ashamed."

Aaron leaned forward, placing his hand on Simon's right knee and said, "don't be ashamed. You are a victim of intimidation, like 99% of your fellow Americans. Fear is what keeps the entire populace in bondage. You are conditioned to fear from the cradle to the grave. You are now facing your fears. Continue your story."

With a look of reassurance on his face, a sense of newfound pride and a determined countenance, Simon now spoke with force and dignity. "So, as I peeped around the corner, Jesus seemed to walk with a more determined and defiant gait, while Matthew appeared to hunch over and walk more hesitantly. As they approached the intersection, those devils from the cars and the sheriff appeared from nooks and crannies with guns drawn. Jesus merely came to a halt, standing there in utter defiance, but Matthew turned and started to run."

As the Son of Thunder

"They must have been afraid of arousing the town with gunfire, so rather than shooting the fleeing Matthew, the woman chased him almost to the alley entrance. I eased myself farther into the shadows, but I saw her catch him and slam her gun butt so hard onto his head that it seemed to crack open as blood spurted out from the wound. She pummelled him as he lay there helpless. She got up and when Matthew turned over seeming to plead for mercy, she place her foot on his chest and push so hard you could hear bones crack. She simply turned, walked back to the others and I shamefully watched Matthew crawl down the sidewalk toward the end of the street, leaving a stream of blood behind him. I am so ashamed of not reaching out to him in his time of need. I knew that there was no hope for him and that he was dying, but he deserved to at least have someone show him some compassion in his final minutes of life."

As Simon wiped away a tear, a compassionate Mary reached out and touched his hand. "Don't fret Simon, my friend Dixon found him before he died, and was there with him when he drew his last breath. He did not die alone."

Reassured, Simon managed a slight smile. He sighed and continued. "When I looked back up the

221

street, Jesus was being pushed into the black SUV. It and the other sedan sped off and the sheriff calmly walked back toward his office. That is the last time I saw Jesus."

So that was it. Perhaps Jesus was still alive. Aaron was now sure that there was a common thread linking the three ministers, the sheriff, the F.B.I. and the N.S.A. to Jesus. There was a light at the end of the proverbial tunnel.

Removing his wallet, Aaron reached in and took out all his cash. It was only $120, but he wanted to give it to Simon. As he offered it to him, Simon waved his hand, indicating he did not want it. Aaron said, "you need it more than I do. I wish I had more to give you. Share it with your friends."

At the same time, Mary removed the $80 she had in her purse and also handed it to Simon, smiling as she said, "it is only money Simon, take it not for yourself, but for us. It makes us feel good to know that we are able to share a little of what we have with those who genuinely need a helping hand."

Without saying a word, Simon accepted the gift with an acknowledging look of appreciation, not just for the money, but for the sentiment behind it.

222

Mary and Aaron got up, walked out of the alley, looked across the street at the magnificent church and realized that the alley of despair behind them harboured far more love than could be found in the monument to intolerance that glistened in the midday sun.

It is not the purpose here to provide love-making details between the 60 year old Aaron and the 36 year old Mary. Rather, this is a chronicle of how Aaron went in search of a man he had never met, but grew to admire him through the many stories about him that others had shared. Yet, no chronicle can be complete without detailing how these two had developed a deep, abiding love that went beyond mere sexual attraction. In fact, it was obvious to Aaron that he could not compete with younger men, and even with most his own age, when it came to looks. However, Mary had seen something in Aaron that made him the most attractive man she had ever met. It had nothing to do with looks, or even sex, it was the purity of Aaron's caring for those marginalized people who had been left behind by a cruel, inhuman system of economic bondage. His rough exterior hid a heart that yearned for some economic and social justice in a world where it was in short supply. Fortunately, his violent streak was reserved for those who preyed upon the weak.

223

With that said, it must be made clear that Aaron's gesture of kindness toward Simon aroused the love Mary felt for him. As they stood on the street, contemplating what they had just experienced, she took his hand in hers, tilted her head and placed it softly on his shoulders and said, "I want to make love to you right now."

Aaron, his newfound libido immediately rising to the occasion and straining against the tightness of his pants, looked about and saw a tiny niche slightly to the right, a few feet into the alleyway. Taking Mary by the hand, he pulled her in, pushed her gently against the wall and passionately kissed her deep, long and hard. Mary seemed to melt in his arms. She whispered softly, "I want you in a special place only reserved for special people."

She turned to face the wall, raising her skirt and placing it against her back to expose her magnificent ass cheeks that were not covered by panties. Putting her head against the stone wall, she jutted her cheeks out, reached down to procure some moisture from her soaking wet love mound and gently placed it where she wanted Aaron's member to plunge deep into her. While she was doing this, Aaron was dropping his pants to his ankles in preparation for what he knew would be quick but passionately mind-blowing sex.

224

The sex only lasted a few seconds as Aaron furiously pounded into her. Yet, it seemed an eternity, as they were wrapped in the rapture of the moment. When it was over, Mary turned and wrapped her arms around Aaron, whispering, "I feel your seed inside me. I want to keep it there forever."

The two lovers felt like high school kids, as they rearranged their clothes and then meandered down Main Street, holding hands. Both knew that the time of reckoning was close at hand. Having left the alley of broken dreams behind, Aaron whispered to her that he would find Jesus no matter what it took. Mary, concerned about Aaron replied, "don't take any chances, my love. I need you so much. I love my friend, but I also love you. I would not want to lose you just to save him."

Aaron turned his head to the right and looked into her eyes. "I am a man who has known more anger than love, more despair than optimism, more sorrow than joy. I thought my life ended years ago, but I have found a new reason to live now. You have given me that, but this man Jesus is the reason I am here. My dearest friend is dead, because he loved this man. I can not rest in your warm arms until I find him."

As the Son of Thunder

A melancholy frown crept across Mary's lips. She slightly lowered her head and sighed. "I know what you must do, and I know you will insist on doing it alone. Please come back to me, Aaron."

Aaron did not verbally reply. He only smiled, grabbed her hand and they continued down the street toward her apartment. The street lights were exceedingly dim and an eerie fog began to creep in from behind them. There was a foreboding quiet all about the street. Then, the moon went behind a cloud and they were bathed in darkness. Aaron assumed it was an ominous sign of coming turmoil.

As the Son of Thunder

CHAPTER 14
THE EVIL, THE EVIL

Their goodbye kiss seemed to linger endlessly the next morning, until finally, when Mary refused to let go of him, Aaron said, "you want to go with me don't you?"

Aaron shook his head in resignation. "It might be dangerous, but if you promise to do as I say, you can come along. I can't be worrying about both you and Jesus. When I find him, there may be violence. And I may only find that he is dead. Are you prepared for that?"

"As long as you are with me, Aaron, I am prepared for anything. Let's go."

How does one find a man who was obviously kidnapped by the U.S. government? Guantanamo Bay was the favourite torture destination for most people deemed terrorists, but from what Aaron had been told and from what he had deduced, it appeared that Jesus was probably still somewhere in New Jersey. Yet, how could he get anyone to lead him to where Jesus was being held? How could he get the authorities and the religious leaders who were obviously in cahoots to reveal what they knew?

227

The sheriff and the three ministers were the best bets to lead him to Jesus. Yet, Aaron was not sure these people knew the exact location. Hell, a little strong arm persuasion and Aaron could probably get any of them to tell him anything they knew. However, not being sure of exactly how much they knew, he decided to start with another visit to the sheriff's office.

Obviously, Agent Shaw, Agent Carter and the NSA jerk, Helpern were most likely privy to Jesus' location, but they would be tougher to handle. On the other hand, if he could spook Sheriff Dillon into getting in touch with the F.B.I. or N.S.A. agents, there might be a chance someone would physically go to the location where Jesus was, and Aaron would follow.

Aaron parked down the street from the sheriff's office and told Mary to wait for him. As he walked into the sheriff's office, the busty blond immediately arose from behind the counter, made a motion with her hand indicating he should stop immediately and said, "hold-on Adams. You aren't welcome around here. You've already caused enough trouble. The sheriff is too busy to see you, anyway. There was a murder last night, and all his time and effort is directed at finding out why someone would kill a bum."

Aaron knew immediately that the bum was Simon. Obviously, he had paid a price for knowing about Jesus' disappearance. The poor guy had been used and discarded by a society with no compassion, and now he had been killed by a pack of government lackey's who saw him as an expendable commodity in their eternal battle against terrorism that existed mostly in the mind. In death, Simon would provide the opening for Aaron to spook Sheriff Dillon into perhaps revealing where Jesus was.

Insisting that he knew something about Simon's death, Aaron made it plain that the sheriff could either see him or that he would be making a beeline to the state attorney general's office. Making sure he said it loud enough for the sheriff to hear through his closed office door, Aaron was not surprised when the sheriff quickly opened his door and said, "get in here Adams."

Giving the busty blond his patented defiance look, Aaron strode into the office and closed the door behind him. The sheriff pointed at a chair, indicating he should sit down, but Aaron said, "I won't be here long enough to sit. I am getting ready to blow the lid off this tin-horn town, and I am bringing you and all your cronies down. You have fucked with the wrong person this time."

229

"If you know anything about Simon's death, you better spill it. As for bringing me and my cronies down, you are way out of your league. You are dealing with the U.S. government."

Aaron placed his hands on the sheriff's desk and leaned slightly forward. "I know that you have no intention of finding out who killed Simon, because you already know who killed him. This is a farce investigation that will be used to cover up what the government assassins did to that poor man. He was murdered, because he told me about seeing Jesus abducted by the government goons who have hidden him away somewhere. He is probably being tortured like anyone else who dares stand-up to the thugs who have been running this country since 9/11. They are the same people who arranged for the murder of my friend Dixon Long, because they were looking for something Jesus gave him. I am on their hit-list, too. The only thing keeping me alive is that they think I might know where that notebook is. Well, send word to those government hoodlums that Aaron Adams has what they are looking for, but they don't have to come after me. I am coming after them, and they better have plenty of firepower, because I am coming with my hands filled."

The sheriff looked perplexed as he eased into his

chair. Aaron slightly grinned, turned and walked out. As he was leaving, he could hear the sheriff banging hard on the telephone keys. Dillon was calling the government boys, and the shit was about to hit the fan. As Aaron made it to the counter, he heard Dillon say, "can't talk on the phone. Will be over in 30 minutes. There's trouble brewing."

Quickly leaving and returning to the car, Aaron motioned for Mary to buckle her seatbelt, as he watched Dillon pull out of the office parking lot and head out of town. Keeping a safe distance, he was shocked at how easy Dillon was making it to follow him.

Driving up the Blackhorse Turnpike, Dillon turned off at the Glassboro exit and drove through the small college town made famous for a summit meeting between Lyndon Johnson and Alexei Kosygin in 1967 at the height of the Cold War. Aaron thought to himself that he was about to go to war, but it would be hot, not cold.

As they left the affluence of the college town, Aaron noticed the landscape begin to change. The streets were more unkempt and the houses seemed older and dilapidated. They were headed toward the slums of Camden.

231

The city was a microcosm of what America had become. On the outside, in the more affluent suburbs, were those residing behind gated estates who had reached the pinnacle of capitalistic success. Then, there were the less affluent, who thought they had attained the good life with their nicely manicured lawns, two cars, a boat, a recreational vehicle and a 3,000 square feet house that they struggled to make payments on each month. Next, were the lower middle class cookie cutter homes, as the change began to be more pronounced. Then, within the city, were those who had been gobbled up and discarded by an economic system that looked on workers as commodities, rather than human beings. These were the lost souls who had to be sacrificed at the altar of greed, so the few could live in luxury.

Mary, sitting quietly as they rode through the slums of despair, looked at Aaron and smiled. Smiling back, Aaron felt a sense of peace surge deep within, as he realized that he no longer walked through life alone. He remembered that he once read that love started with a smile, grows with a kiss and ends with a tear. He had been through that with his beloved B.J. many years ago, and had given up on love, because of the tears she had caused. Now, Mary had given him the opportunity to walk from the darkness he had been

232

locked in so long into the bright sunshine of happiness. Yet, their vast age difference bothered him. Sensing he was in deep thought about their relationship, Mary said, "don't be so pensive, Aaron. We are going to stay together, because I see in you all I have ever wanted in a man."

Aaron, pleased at what she said, but still apprehensive, replied, "but our age difference could one day become a problem, if it already isn't one. I am 60 years old, and the way I have lived probably only gives me a few years more of life."

Mary, her eyes glowing brightly and a smile creeping across her face, said, "love is not a matter of counting the years. It is making the years count. Whether I have twenty years or twenty minutes left, I want to spend them with you."

Aaron, not looking at Mary, as he was concentrating on staying a safe distance from Sheriff Dillon, said nonchalantly, "you are proof that love has nothing to do with what you are expecting to get, only with what you are expecting to give. You, Mary, have given me everything I thought was gone forever."

Not uttering a word, Mary simply reached over and placed her hand on Aaron's right thigh. There

233

As the Son of Thunder

was no need for words.

Dillon turned down an avenue of broken dreams, with dilapidated tenements lining both sides of the street, and people wandering aimlessly on the sidewalks with that blank stare that is a hallmark of those who have lost all hope in a society where poverty is the price paid to coddle and protect the rich and powerful.

As the daylight began to subside, there was a police chopper circling overhead in the distance, and the eerie sound of the rotor blades slapping through the thick, humid air seemed to be playing a melancholic concerto of misery in the slum that was used to imprison those sacrificed at the altar of greed. People huddled under steps or lay in doorways, because they had been denied the dignity of a roof over their heads.

Looking about them at the human misery wrought by materialism, Aaron and Mary glanced briefly at one another and sighed. Aaron thought to himself that if there was a God, he would love to meet him face-to-face and give him a piece of his mind for allowing the few to live in luxurious splendour while relegating so many to a banal existence where they had to beg for crumbs from the exalted rich assholes who lived in splendour.

As the Son of Thunder

Dillon turned right at an intersection and headed toward the Delaware River area that primarily consisted of derelicts sleeping under the bridges, families using abandoned cars as homes and individuals with make-shift card-board boxes shielding them from the elements. They passed a soup kitchen where the line was already a block long as people queued up for their evening meal and a dose of Jesus for dessert. Aaron thought to himself, "welcome to the new world order."

Staying twenty car lengths behind Dillon, Aaron looked to his right and saw a woman bathing a baby in the river. These people were so lucky to be living in the promised land, where everyone is equal. Aaron wondered when all these people with holes in their bellies would eventually get the courage to put a gun in their hands and demand justice. Meanwhile, the ministers were telling them that the meek would inherit the earth, and the day was coming when the last shall be first and the first shall be last. What a joke. The ministers were part of the privileged class and kept those they were supposed to serve in chains by feeding them tall-tales about a man born of a virgin. People were just as simple minded today as they were in the Dark Ages. The world was still run by the lords of the manor while the serfs begged for sustenance. What had changed?

235

Passing through the underbelly of the city, seeing nothing but ruined building after building with uniformly broken or ill-fitting windows, and the incredible state of filth from the piled debris and refuse, Aaron and Mary felt like they were in some third world cesspool. The standing pools of dirty water all about emitted a stench that penetrated through the rolled-up windows of the car. How could a society call itself civilized and allow its citizens to live in such squalor?

Suddenly, Dillon made a right turn onto a dirt road with no street lights. Aaron followed, but turned off his lights so the sheriff would not pick up the glare in his rear view mirror. The horrors of poverty were all about them. The street was lined with scraggy, thin-as-a-rail men and women dressed in tattered clothing. They wandered about aimlessly with glazed looks, lost in a dense jungle of despair. Aaron and Mary felt as if they had penetrated the chaos perpetrated by a society where greed ruled supreme. These people were the result of a diseased economic system that let all the good things flow to the top while ignoring those at the bottom. How could a society that called itself just allow this evil to exist in the midst of plenty? When would the poor finally arm themselves and march into the gated estates of their jailers and demand justice?

Dillon continued down the road until the human squalor faded. All that was left was torn down buildings. The debris had been neatly stacked in the centre of the lots, obviously in order to make sure there was a vast open area to make it easy to spot any intruders. A huge chain link fence at least 20 feet high, that was, no doubt, electrified and had razor wire on the top, encased a huge area that backed onto the river. Dillon pulled up at a gate toward the end of the road, and two armed guards waved him in, after he apparently showed them some identification. Aaron pulled to the side of the road about 1000 feet from the gate to avoid any chance of detection. He and Mary looked at each other quizzically, but did not utter a word.

Thinking about what to do, Aaron finally broke the silence. "This is, no doubt, a government facility, and Jesus might just be here. Getting in is not going to be easy. I want you to get behind the wheel of the car and keep the motor running. No matter what happens, don't fret too much. I have gotten into more secure places than this many times. When you see me coming out the gate, drive like hell up to it. Reach around and open the back door so we can dive in. Don't bother to close it, just slam down on the accelerator, make a u-turn and head back the way we came. In all likelihood there will be total chaos. Ignore it."

With a determined look, Mary replied, "got it. Be careful, Aaron."

Aaron got out and gingerly walked behind the dilapidated buildings on the right side of the street, being careful to avoid detection. There were no lights on around the compound, but as he moved toward the gate, he saw a long driveway with dim lights that led up to a huge, old grey house in the distance. Tall hedges guarded a gate, behind which were two men with machine guns. Looking to his left, Aaron saw the debris that had been piled into the centre. He knew it wasn't just debris, it was a cover for guard towers that were hidden within the piles. Although he could not see them, he knew from his military experience that there were snipers behind the debris with infra-red sites probably scanning the area continuously. Feeling a sense of exhilaration from the adrenalin pumping rapidly through his body , he felt like he was a much younger man. He had been a trained killer in the military, but that was a long-time ago. He was up against younger men who had been brainwashed much better than he was. These were men who were convinced through psychological manipulation that all things were permissible when done in defence of liberty. They had no compunction about killing anyone who stood in America's way.

238

Working his way behind the façade of a building that had been gutted, he slowly removed his jacket and adjusted his shoulder holster, making sure that his gun was easily accessible. He reached down into a pool of water and brought out a huge hand full of mud that he smeared over the front and back of his white shirt. He coated his face with the mud until he felt he was basically undetectable in the darkness. Peaking around the corner of the building, he lowered himself to the ground and began methodically crawling on his belly towards the hedges at the gate. Once there, he lay quietly for a few seconds so close to the guards that he could hear them breathing. With no silencer for his gun, he knew that he had to eliminate them silently with his hands, but getting them outside the gate would be impossible. As he was thinking about his next move, a car pulled up to the gate and one of the guards opened it and stepped out to the car. As he was talking to the driver, Aaron crawled undetected to the back of the car, slid under it, removed his belt and wrapped it around a piece of metal, holding on tightly as the car pulled through the gate, dragging him under it toward the house. As stones cut into his back, the pain forced him to release his grip and he lay precariously in the driveway for a few seconds before rolling out of sight behind some nearby shrubs.

As the Son of Thunder

Wincing from the pain in his back, Aaron got to his feet and duck-walked his way toward the house in order to avoid detection. The house had been a magnificent edifice many years ago. It overlooked the river from the rear. Several willow trees lined the side where Aaron huddled. Not too smart he thought, as they half concealed the house, making it possible for anyone who could get passed the guards to use them to hide from view. Moss and ivy covered the walls, seeming to cling to the ruins of the old estate as if embracing an evil that lurked within.

Slowly working his way in a zigzag fashion behind the shrubs toward the back of the mansion to avoid detection from the video cameras, Aaron could hear the river washing against the stone covered shore that was within a few feet of the screened-in back porch. Several willow trees in the back of the house had grown so tall and wide that the branches were banging gently against the roof, as a slight breeze with intense dampness came off the shore of the river. Half concealing the back porch, the trees were a perfect hiding place. Aaron crawled along the path that was overgrown with weeds until he was behind the giant trunk of one of the trees. Waiting patiently, he methodically surveyed the huge screened-in back porch, contemplating his next move.

240

Looking at the once stately mansion that had at one time, no doubt, been the estate of a turn-of-the-century robber baron, Aaron glanced to his right and saw a dilapidated arbour, where there was a rotting table that time had not quite destroyed. To the back of the arbour was a plot of land that had once been an elaborate garden. All about there was an intense sadness to the place, making one feel like being in a graveyard and reading from ancient tombstones. This was a place of more than mere confinement for the man calling himself Jesus. It was a monument to insidious evil.

The cold breeze seemed to bite through to the bone, as if preparing Aaron to face the malignancy of what lay within. He crawled to the back porch, making sure to stay behind the shrubs. Once to the door, he inched up the three steps on his belly. The screen door was not even latched. He eased it open and crawled onto the grey painted wooden back porch and looked up at a huge steel door. There was no way he could get through it, but he might get someone to open it and get the jump on them when they did.

Looking above the door, he saw a few boards loose in the ceiling. He looked to his right and saw a chair and a table with an ashtray on it. Stealthily

241

moving the table near the door, he reached up and removed a few lose boards. Pulling himself up by gripping the studs above him, he eased himself into the opening that was only an arm's length from the door. He reached down and pounded as hard as he could on the steel door. Almost instantly, it sprang open, and out stepped a bulky man with a revolver in his right hand. Scanning the porch, the lone gunman looked confused.

Aaron dropped down from the rafters feet first, wrapping his legs around the man's neck and reaching down to knock the gun out of his hand. Gripping tightly, he strangled the man with his legs until they both fell to the floor. Aaron, sitting on the man's back, with his feet still wrapped around his neck, hit him several blows in the back of the head, and he felt him go limp.

Immediately rolling off the bulky frame, pulling his 45 and glancing back, Aaron assumed a crouching position, expecting another guard to be spitting lead. There was no one, just an empty kitchen. He reached down and felt the man's pulse. There was nothing.

Going inside, he looked to his right and noticed steps leading to a cellar. Easing down the stairs with his 45 cocked and ready,he cautiously moved

As the Son of Thunder

toward what appeared to be a cavernous chamber that was completely encased in thick blackened iron. A sliding steel door had been left wide open. He could not help but ask himself why it was so easy to get into the place?

The dim lights cast an eerie glow all about the room, but no matter how dim the lights, Aaron realized that you did not have to see the evil. You could feel it. You could smell it. And the coldness seemed to penetrate right to the heart.

To his left, against a wall, lit by a small wattage bulb that slightly flickered, was an infamous medieval rack with metal rollers that were used to stretch the body. There were urine and feces stains on the metal bed upon which a victim would be stretched. One could almost hear the sounds of tendons being ripped, joints separated and bones fracturing. Aaron felt nauseous.

Gazing slightly to the right of the rack, he saw wooden posts with iron staples for holding heavy weights. Hanging off them were thick iron shackles, stained with blood. The wicker steps beneath the posts were, no doubt, kicked out from under the victim to inflict excruciating pain from dangling three feet off the floor. The sickness of it repulsed Aaron. How could human beings do this

243

to one another?

In the corner was an iron torture chair, studded with a long, thick, bulbous, penis-like device right in the middle, probably used to insert up the anus of the person sitting in the chair. It included stocks for the feet that extended over an open pit that probably would have hot coals in it to scorch the feet.

Almost to the point of vomiting at the horror before him, Aaron looked a bit further to his right and there it was, the Dick Cheney special, the infamous water-boarding table. Sitting atop it was a funnel for pressing down the throat to force water into the victim. No, this wasn't torture. It was only the legitimate use of repetitive force as defined by the Bush Administration. Call it by another name, and it isn't torture according to the minions who justified the unjustifiable.

Lowering his head, Aaron had to fight back tears. How could this place exist in the USA? How could the American people have allowed their government to stoop so low? How could a country that held itself up as a beacon for the rest of the world resort to this in the name of security? Where did they find the people willing to carry-out this evil? The evil, the evil.....................

CHAPTER 15
WEEP FOR HUMANITY

Aaron did not see the man. He only heard the soft, almost whispery voice coming from the darkness to his right. The words seemed to reverberate all about the chamber. "We have been expecting you Mr. Adams. Dillon made it easy for you to follow him. Too bad you killed the guard. It wasn't necessary. Shaw, Helpern and Dillon knew that it would take a man of my talents to get you to reveal where the notebook is. Yes, we know that you have it. That you took it from Dixon Long's, and that you are responsible for the deaths of the two agents at his house. We have had an agent watching your office ever since you got back from Arkansas. We have searched your office, your car, your apartment, but it seems you have done a good job of hiding it. Well, I am, like you, good at my job, and I can assure you that you will eventually tell me where it is."

Slowly raising his head in the direction the voice was coming from, Aaron replied, "you don't know me very well then. I'm not telling you anything. You are the one who is going to do the talking. I am going to ask you just once where Jesus is. Then, if I don't get the answer I want, this fucking place is going to be filled with your screams. You

245

will be begging me to kill you. If I get what I want, I may just do it quick and relatively pain-free. If you are stupid enough not to give me what I want, your little chamber of horrors here is going to be a monument to cruelty, and you are going to be the statue that commemorates the pain one man can inflict on another.

The room was suddenly bathed in light, and standing by the light switch was an incredibly tall man with a dark face and considerable breadth to his chest. He had stern features, a heavy brow and his eyes were dark and intense. He was probably in his mid-thirties. He did not have the look of a torturer, rather, he could have passed for a mild-mannered accountant. He was immaculately dressed in grey slacks and a sport shirt with a silk scarf about his neck that was neatly tucked under the open collar. A smile slowly crept across his lips, showing a slight gap between his front teeth. This was the new face of torture in the modern world. He was a specialist.

Levelling his gun at the man, Aaron thought he had the upper hand, but just then, behind him, he heard the click of several guns as they were being cocked. The tall man smiled again and said, "drop your gun, Mr. Adams. You may have a gun, but I have control of the situation."

As the Son of Thunder

Glancing over his right shoulder, Aaron saw three men with revolvers levelled right at him. He was at a disadvantage and he knew it. He dropped his gun.

Again, that smile slowly crept across the man's face. "I am Otto. I hope you will refuse to tell me where the notebook is, because I am a man who enjoys his work. Just telling me right away makes my job too easy."

The voice was calm, melodic and intense. Yet, it reverberated all about the room like a shockwave. It seemed to open the doors to hell, and Aaron knew he was about to find out what hell was like. He was looking at Satan. The light was bright in the chamber, but Aaron was still surrounded by darkness.

Ignoring Aaron's gun on the floor, Otto and the four gunmen escorted Aaron to a nearby sofa. Gesturing with his right index finger for Aaron to have a seat, Otto pulled up a wooden chair, sit down, crossed his legs and let that insidious smile creep across his lips once again. Rubbing his lower lip with his left index finger and thumb, Otto said, "you will die Mr. Adams. That I promise you. Like you offered me, I am offering you the choice of how you die."

247

Aaron's mind raced with thoughts of how to escape. There would be no mercy from these men. He knew that Otto had refined cruelty to an art-form in this chamber of horrors. Aaron was a strong man, and had endured captivity twice in Vietnam, but even he had his breaking point. He knew he had much to fear, because Otto was a product of a new type of government that produced robots who were brainwashed into patriotic servitude in the belief that all was justified in defence of so-called liberty. Yet, ask these auto-bots what liberty was, and they could not even define it.

Thinking of Mary, who was waiting for him, made Aaron's heart sink. Time seem suspended, as he gazed about the room with an air of doubt and amazement. For an instance, he lamented the visions of happiness that were now vanishing as he recoiled from the inevitability of his predicament. Yet, as he surveyed the gloomy dungeon of despair, a calm overcame him, a serene acceptance of his fate. But what of Mary, sweet Mary?

That smile, that evil smile crept across Otto's lips again. It started in the left corner with the lips parting ever so slightly, then expanding as it crept toward the middle of his mouth.

248

As the Son of Thunder

Almost laughing out loud now, Otto said, "I know what you are thinking, but believe me, there is no escape. That pious, self-righteous, proverb spouting hypocrite calling himself Jesus thought he could escape by playing on our emotions, but we knew that he was nothing but a terrorist masquerading as a holy man. I put him on the rack, hung him in shackles, water-boarded him a few times and he screamed like any other man would. He's no son of God. He was pretty strong though. He refused to tell us where the notebook was. He is in cold storage right now. My favourite way to get terrorists to talk is putting them in the freezer naked for a few hours. That way, I don't have to clean up any blood or piss off the floor. That is where that asshole Jesus is now. I think I will let you join him."

As Otto finished, he glanced to his left at an open door that led into a hallway. Aaron sensed that was where he would find Jesus, if he was still alive. First, he had to figure out how to kill four men when he had no gun.

Immediately, Aaron stood up and then dropped to his knees. Grabbing both of Otto's feet, he pulled him down under him, straddling his stomach, as he looked up at the three gunmen who had their revolvers aimed right at him.

249

As the Son of Thunder

Otto shouted, "wound him, don't kill him. We need the notebook."

With his hands tightly around Otto's neck, he rolled over, pulling Otto on top of him. He could feel Otto convulsing as bullets riddled his body. Looking to his right, Aaron saw his 45 still on the floor. He summoned all his strength and hurled Otto's lifeless body toward the gunmen who made the mistake of standing side-by-side. The body fell at their feet and caused a momentary lapse in their shooting spree.

Rolling across the floor, Aaron felt bullets whizzing underneath his body, slightly tearing into his flesh. Grasping his gun on the floor, he continued to roll until he was under the water board table. While on his back, he placed his feet in the middle of the table and turned it over, giving him temporary cover.

One of the men said, "you two go around the right and left. Me and Curt will go straight ahead. Remember, just wound him."

He should not have said it so loud, because now Aaron was prepared. He had an advantage, because they were not shooting to kill, but Aaron was. He sat with his back to the table, waiting for

As the Son of Thunder

them, waiting to spit death from his big bastard of a 45.

They all arrived almost simultaneously. Aaron saw the guy on the left out of the corner of his eye and shot him on the bridge of the nose before he could squeeze off a round. A bullet whizzed by Aaron from the right, and he leaned back, pulling the trigger as he lay prone on the floor. Aaron's bullet went through the left eye of the man, projecting upward, causing brain matter to explode out of the back of his head.

One of the other men cautiously leaned over the table, gun hand extended. Aaron, still lying on his back and looking straight up, shot him right below the left shoulder. As the gunman continued firing, he fell on the edge of the table. Aaron shot him in the forehead, and he went limp on the table edge.

Then, Aaron heard a stern voice. "You asshole, that is six shoots. You're done for. You're going to tell me where the notebook is, and then I'm going to kill you with my bare hands."

Aaron lay there on the floor, looking up at the ceiling, gun still in his hand, breathing heavily. The gunman walked around the left side of the table. Standing at the end of the overturned table,

251

he looked down at Aaron, holstered his gun and said, "I am going to enjoy this. After you tell me where the notebook is, you are going to beg me to kill you, but I won't, not until you have genuinely paid for this carnage."

Aaron looked up at him and said, "you stupid government asshole. I've got a 1911 Colt 45. They hold seven bullets, not six."

The bastard tried to reach for his holstered gun, but he was already a dead man. Smiling, Aaron pulled the trigger and blew a huge hole in the middle of his forehead. He collapsed over a table leg, broke it and fell onto the floor with his head resting on Aaron's outstretched left leg. Aaron kicked the lifeless body aside, got to his feet and headed down the open door and a corridor that would lead to Jesus, saying out loud, "this is for you Dixon, old friend."

Thick iron walls also lined the corridor, making the chamber a place where the tortured could only hear their own screams and the screams of those other poor souls suffering at the hands of the servants of the true Satan. And it was not the horn-headed demon of the Bible, it was the U.S. government itself that was the modern day Satan, using evil to fight evil.

252

Reaching into his pant's pocket for ammunition, Aaron reloaded the 45, while walking down the corridor toward a steel door at the end.

As he got to the door, he looked though the narrow plated glass window and saw three naked bodies lying on gurneys. He had never heard a description of Jesus, but looking down at the long-haired, bearded man on the middle gurney, he immediately knew it was the man who had caused so much turmoil in a small New Jersey town. He could see why Mary and Dixon had been so taken with him. There was an aura about him, as he lay there between two other men. Was Aaron too late? All three appeared dead.

As Aaron pulled the latch to open the freezer door, the man on the middle gurney rose up and smiled. Sitting with his stiffened legs dangling off the edge of the gurney, he said, "what took you so long?"

Shocked by the greeting, Aaron replied, "you know who I am?"

Again, smiling as he got to his feet, Jesus said, "of course, you are Dixon's dear friend, Aaron Adams. You look just as he described you. Any chance we could find me some clothes and get out

253

As the Son of Thunder

out of this devil's den of inequity?"

As Aaron quizzically looked at the other two men, Jesus said, "they are beyond your help, Aaron. Although one was completely innocent, the other was guilty of many acts defined by the government as terrorism. Yet, for him, it was justifiable retaliation for what he considered terrorism by America.. All terrorism is in the eye of the beholder. To paraphrase Che Guevara, one man's terrorist is another man's freedom fighter."

Mesmerized by the serenity of this man, Aaron was almost speechless, but managed to unintelligibly utter, "let's get out of here," as he reached out to touch Jesus' arm with his right hand.

Raising his right hand and waving it to indicate Aaron should not touch him, Jesus said, "do not touch me my friend, I am still bitterly cold. I have been in here for awhile."

Aaron said, "Yeah, I am just glad I was able to get to you in time. You couldn't have lasted much longer. You are ghostly white now."

Letting a grin slowly sweep across his lips, Jesus replied, "Yes, I am the ghost of righteousness."

Removing the clothes from one of the dead gunmen and handing them to Jesus, Aaron said, "next, we have to figure our way out of here."

Putting on the clothes, as he pointed to a small vestibule to the left of the chamber, Jesus said, "there are the cameras. Disconnect them and it will give us an advantage. I, like you, am here to stand against tyranny, and sometimes, when faced with no other choice, those who try to halt injustice must realize that only by spilling blood can the sanctity of man be protected. This is, no doubt, one of those times."

Aaron disconnected the cameras, came back, took two guns from the dead bodies and offered one to Jesus. Shaking his head left to right, Jesus said, "don't you know I have the power to destroy enemies with the mere wave of a hand? I am a supreme being."

Sighing, Aaron replied, "so, why were you in cold storage?"

Almost laughing, Jesus said, "good question Aaron? But I still think I will pass on the gun."

Tucking the two guns in his belt, Aaron motioned for Jesus to follow him. As they went up

255

the stairs, Jesus looked back for a fleeting moment at the room where his agonizing ordeal had made him painfully aware that a contaminated political environment had made illegal arrest, detention and torture acceptable in a society gripped with fear. How could those who professed a belief in Christ think that maiming minds and bodies would be an acceptable way for a just society to operate? The evil of that room represented the evil in the hearts of all who served tyranny.

Stepping onto the back porch, Aaron whispered, "stick close to me. Mary will meet us at the gate."

Nonchalantly, Jesus said, "of course she will, and from the tone of your voice, I would say she is waiting more for you than me. I am glad the two of you found each other."

Mystified at how he could possibly know about their relationship. Aaron replied, "you are a pretty perceptive fellow. If I was religious, I might actually believe you were the son of God."

"You don't need to be religious, and you don't need to believe that I am the son of God. All you have to do is stand for justice in a world where there is none. Get me out of here, and I shall continue my work to right wrongs."

256

As they stepped off the back porch and crouched low, staying hidden behind the shrubs, Aaron pointed toward the gate about 200 feet away. "When I start firing, run like hell for the gate. Don't look back, just move your ass. Mary will pull up to the gate when she hears the gunfire."

Nodding in the affirmative, Jesus' eyes met Aaron's. The mutual respect was evident. Aaron stood up straight and with the two guns he had confiscated from the dead men, he fired three rounds at the guards in the distance. The guards were so surprised that they could not pivot their guns and fire before they were riddled with bullets and fell convulsing violently to the ground. Aaron, running frantically behind Jesus, never looked back until he got to the gate, turned and saw Sheriff Dillon running from the house, firing relentlessly at him. Feeling a bullet crease his right ear, he kept pulling the triggers as Jesus undid the gate and Mary pulled up with the engine racing frantically. Watching the sheriff fall head first onto the ground, mortally wounded, Aaron kept pulling the triggers until they clicked onto empty chambers. He dropped them, turned and dived into the back seat of the car, just as Jesus was sitting up. Mary made a quick u-turn and headed back up the street. There was no fire from anywhere else. They had made it.

257

Leaning forward, Jesus whispered, "hello Mary. You are a hell of a driver."

They all let out a laugh as Jesus continued, "take me to the metro station in Camden. I have a train to catch."

Meanwhile, back at the compound laid waste by Aaron, a flurry of activity was taking place. Agent Carter, Agent Shaw and Agent Helpern arrived together to survey the carnage. Having underestimated Aaron's abilities, they were surprised to see the sheriff had been killed and their prime prisoner removed by Aaron Adams.

Obviously, the whole place would have to be abandoned in order to cover up what had been going on there. Contacting Washington, a cover story was already being prepared by higher-ups to satisfy the news media that would, no doubt, soon be nosing around the old, abandoned estate in Camden. It was decided to cover-up the whole episode by burning the entire estate to the ground and indicating that the government had cornered a group of terrorists who had set up a bomb factory in an old mansion. The terrorists died in a fire they set themselves, after killing a local sheriff and several government agents. The public would easily swallow the story, and it could even be used to galvanize public opinion once again in the fight against the evil-doers who were trying to destroy the American way of life. As Hitler said, "the bigger the lie, the more likely people are to believe it."

Carter made a frantic call to New York City and talked to a female agent there, telling her to meet them outside Aaron's office, because they assumed he would be returning to the city, and whether they found the notebook or not, it was now imperative they eliminate him and Mary Madison. He, Shaw and Helpern would be driving up almost immediately.

Pulling into the Camden train station, Jesus looked at Aaron and said, "I guess you know that someone is going to have to buy me a ticket, because I have no money."

Aaron, smilingly replied, "from what I hear, you never have any money."

As Mary turned to look at the two men in the back seat, Jesus exhibited his usual, calm demeanour as he said, "I have never had any servants. Yet, people call me master. I have never had a university degree, but people call me teacher. I have no medicines, but people call me a

259

healer. I have never had any money, but I am rich, because I call people like you and Mary, friend."

Aaron, ever the pessimist replied, "I am not sure I can afford many friends like you. Come on in, and I will buy you a ticket on my credit card."

As they walked toward the station, Mary started to reach for Jesus' hand, but he immediately stopped her and said, "I am still cold, do not touch me now, as I want you to remember the warmth we shared in our time together."

Asking Jesus where he was headed, Aaron felt like he was about to lose a dear friend forever. Jesus, his eyes twinkling like bright stars in the night, replied, "I can only take the train as far as Seattle. From there, I shall slip across the Canadian border and make my way to a small island off the British Columbia coast, where Aboriginals still live a simple life free of materialism. It is there that I will recuperate and connect with those who still know compassion. When the time is right, I shall emerge again, and try once more to bring light to the darkness.

A train was due to leave in only ten minutes. Buying the ticket for him, Aaron walked stoically with Jesus and Mary down the platform toward the

260

train. Seeing that they were both despondent about his departure, Jesus offered solace in words of wisdom. "Memory is the treasury and guardian of all things. It lets you hold onto the things you love. We do not remember days. We remember moments. Memories are footprints on the heart. Do not lament my leaving. Smile because we had time together. Life is not measured by the number of breaths you take, but by the number of moments that take your breath away. We shall forever live in one another's hearts."

"I know you have my notebook, Aaron. I leave the two of you with an admonition to see that my words as scribed in that book reach the right people. I suggest the *New York Times*. What lies ahead for the two of you will not be easy. Remember that if there is no struggle there is no progress. Those who profess to love freedom, but are unwilling to fight for it, make slaves of themselves. You cannot grow crops without ploughing the ground first. You cannot have rain without occasional thunder and lightning."

As the conductor yelled "all aboard," Jesus smiled and walked down the platform. Turning and looking back over his right shoulder, smiling broadly at the two morose friends, his parting words seemed to reverberate all about the station.

261

"Do not worry about living long years, but worry about living the years you have well. All things move onward, nothing abides. Live the present moments, so that in the end you can say you made the most of every day."

Jesus, now, himself seeming a bit sullen, his voiced slightly cracking with emotion, lowered his head a bit, and a tear slowly trickled down his right cheek. "Whenever you see a cop beating a demonstrator. Whenever you see the hungry crying for a crumb from the table of plenty. Whenever you see the jails filled with those who stand against injustice. Whenever you see people beg for a job or struggling for a place to rest their heads. Whenever you see people labouring valiantly to be free. Look deep, long and hard into their eyes. You will see me. I am always with those who seek justice where there is none."

As he walked up the steps into the car, he stopped and looked back at Aaron and Mary once more as the train began to pull away. Seeing Mary place her head on Aaron's shoulder as she wept, his final words, somewhat muffled by the sound of the engine, were "I have been crucified many times, and I shall be crucified again. Weep not for me, weep for humanity."

262

As the Son of Thunder

CHAPTER 16
BUT A SWORD

Aaron was in some pain from his minor wounds, but refused to see a doctor, as he was intent on getting back to his office as soon as possible, recovering the notebook and getting it to the *New York Times* to expose the hypocritical conspiracy.

Just as Aaron and Mary were making their way into Manhattan, Annie was pushing her cart hurriedly down the sidewalk in front of Aaron's office. Stopping beneath his window, and parking the cart at an angle against the building, she looked up and saw that the window was open. No lights were on, and even though the window was slightly above eye level, elevating herself on her toes, she could see that no one was there.

Agents Carter, Shaw and Helpern cruised by Aaron's office in the black sedan and pulled around the corner to park out-of-sight in the alley-way. Walking up to Sidewalk Annie, they greeted her with a nod. Carter said, "is he here, yet?"

"No, the place is empty," replied Annie as she briskly moved with the three stoic men toward the entrance to the building. She looked at Helpern and said, "let's nail this son-of-bitch."

263

Going through the revolving doors, Aaron's office was to the right. Carter pointed to a broom closet in the hallway, where all four sequestered themselves in delightful anticipation of the coming battle.

The door slightly ajar, so they could easily see when Aaron entered the building, in their minds each individual was going over the reasons why the coming barbarity was justified. After all, they were guardians of freedom, and extremism in defence of liberty was no vice in their brainwashed minds. Not comprehending the inequity, exploitive nature and indifference of the nation, they felt as if they were the vanguards in the struggle between good and evil. They could not see that the use of evil to fight evil made them accomplices in the crimes of those they served.

These four people were lost souls in a sea of deceit, but they could not comprehend the depths of depravity to which they had acquiescently acceded in order to protect the nation from a man deemed a terrorist by terrorists. They could not grasp the irony of a man preaching love, compassion and kindness for the marginalized of the world being labelled a threat to the peace and harmony of the nation. They were just four more clueless pawns willing to serve the interests of the rich and powerful.

The closet was hot and stuffy. All four of them were perspiring profusely. Each, in their own minds, was going over the justifications for what was about to occur.

Helpern was the biggest of the three men hiding in the closet, and his stern demeanour complimented his unyielding dedication to protecting what he always referred to as the American way. Coming from an upper middle class family, he thought that those at the bottom of the economic ladder were simply mooching off the hard-working people like him and his parents. To him, this Jersey Jesus was no modern day messiah. He was just a con-man trying to stir up a group of people who were wanting a hand-out. To top it off, Aaron Adams was a left-wing radical posing as a do-gooder who wanted to question the sanctity of the best economic system in the world. These two men and that whore were just malcontents who wanted to destroy the country. What they were about to get was well-deserved, and he would feel no remorse in doing what was necessary to remove the evil they represented.

Carter was the shortest of the three men, with muscular features and a jutting chin that made him

265

appear to be foreboding, uncompromising and disciplined. His eyebrows were thick and bushy, and they flicked up and down as he thought about what had led to this moment in his life. Only 28, he had, from childhood, been conditioned by school, church and his parents to never question authority. To him, there was a natural order to things, and those who questioned that order stood against God and country. Now, as a member of the F.B.I., he was vociferously committed to making sure that the evil-doers were brought to justice, and Mary and Aaron Adams were accomplices to this evil-doer calling himself by a name reserved for the one and only true Christ. Pulling the trigger and despatching these devils to rot in eternal damnation was a task he welcomed and embraced. There would be no remorse for destroying those who served the devil.

The white-haired Shaw was the most distinguished looking of the group sent to retrieve the notebook and dispatch Aaron and Mary. In his mid-forties, he could have easily passed for a university professor, but beneath that academic looking exterior was a malevolent, cold, stern heart. He was looking forward to bringing down Aaron for exhibiting such disdain for the authority he represented. How could any loyal American question the authority of the F.B.I.?

266

As the Son of Thunder

Finally, there was Sidewalk Annie, real name, Anita Longworth. At 40, in her carefully administered makeup, missing teeth black bridge and dishevelled wig, she looked at least 60. Oddly, of the four government agents, she was the most misanthropic, harsh and cold-blooded. When she received the call from the Arkansas F.B.I. office about the death of the two agents, she felt that her special skills at impersonation would be vital in exacting justice on Aaron Adams. Donning the garb of a street person, she was able to keep a close eye on what was going on in Aaron's office. She had ransacked the place in a futile effort to find the notebook. Now, she felt unrestrained. She and the other three had been given the green light to eradicate this malignancy, notebook or no notebook.

These four saw themselves as holy warriors of righteousness. Yet, in true evil they delighted. They had been deceived and manipulated by a power structure that needed an obedient brainwashed army of devotees to invoke their insidious, inhumane, contemptible system of servitude. They were too indoctrinated in service to a bankrupt ideal to realize that they were maligning the righteous and dispossessing the wise by planning to eradicate Aaron and Mary. Turning their backs on the good represented by the

267

son of man, they were ridiculing and scorning reason and virtue. Observing the kindness and purity of a man worthy of praise, they were suppressing the truth. They invented and circulated vile talk, traducing and slandering the innocent while they rejected the good and embraced the evil. These four harboured and kept treacherous hearts that were beating with disdain for all those who stood against what they had been taught to believe.

"Woe unto the world because of offences, for it is necessary that offences will cometh, but woe to the man by whom offences cometh." (Matthew 18:7)

It was raining, and the wipers were making a soft, whirring noise as Aaron and Mary entered the Bowery. Ripples of water radiated in intersecting waves as they cascaded down the windshield. The sun had just gone down and the lights of the city were welcoming the dark with shades of red, white, blue and yellow. The sidewalks seemed to glitter with the jewels of raindrops. Everything appeared quiet and peaceful, even in this underbelly of the city, where hopelessness and despair stood in glaring contrast to other parts of Manhattan. Yet, they both sensed that the peace and tranquility were illusionary.

268

There was a sudden flash of lightning that lit up the cloudy sky. Thunder followed and seemed to reverberate off the buildings on each side of the street. Mary reached over and took Aaron's right hand, squeezing it tightly.

They sensed what was coming could be catastrophic. Yet, it was, as if together, they were a formable force in the fight against tyranny. Without complexities or pride, they knew that neither had really existed before they found one another. They could turn around and leave the city. They could find a place where they would be safe and sheltered from the terror they were about to face. Neither could speak of it though, because they both felt a duty to this person calling himself Jesus and to Dixon Long, a friend who had died in defence of this man.

"The majority of people lead quiet, unheralded lives. Most will have no monuments erected to honour them. There will be no front page headlines for most people. In fact, most will not even make the back pages of the newspaper, until their obituaries are written. But that does not lessen their impact, as there are scores of people out there looking for a hand up from a compassionate person. An individual can live a happier life simply because someone cared. Never

269

underestimate the power of one person to make a difference. Do not disparage the power of a smile, a touch, a compliment, a willingness to listen or the smallest act of kindness, because they all have the power to change a person's life." (Jesus in Woodbury Creek, New Jersey, 2006).

Aaron and Mary were two people who were shining examples of what those words spoken by Jesus in 2006 meant, but Aaron was also an avenging angel when dealing with those who had no mercy or compassion. He refused to go quietly into the night and bow at the altar of religious subterfuge and patriotic babble that was used to enslave people to an idea that was as bankrupt as the government in Washington that served the interests of the few at the expense of the many.

Jesus had suffered at the hands of those who feared the truth. Now, it was up to Aaron and Mary to see that his story got out. It was time the world knew the real Jesus. Even though Aaron was not convinced of his divinity, he was sure that this was a good and just man who had been put upon mercilessly by a system that wanted to crush those who dared defy authority. Aaron, himself, had often known the consequences of defying authority. For that reason, he had a real kinship with Jesus.

270

"Behold, I will send you Elijah the prophet before the coming of that great and dreadful day of the Lord. And he shall turn the heart of the fathers to the children, lest I come and smite the earth with a curse." (Malachi 4:5-6)

In his own way, Aaron was a modern-day Elijah, a man unafraid and un-bowing before those who tried to keep the masses in chains. He understood that the people of his nation were tightly secured in invisible chains as they meekly submitted to injustice after injustice. He knew that the limits of tyrants were prescribed by the endurance of those they oppressed, and America was a nation of meek lambs that wilfully lined up to be led to slaughter.

Aaron's office was in one of the least desirable areas of lower Manhattan, but it was just on the edge of an area of respectability. He was there, because the rent was cheap and it was close enough to the wealthy enclaves to allow him to attract an upscale clientele. The route he was taking took them through the underbelly of the city, a sea of misery in an island of affluence. It was a stark example of how greed ruled supreme in a land of broken promises. Aaron thought to himself that there could be no privileged class without the suffering of the lower class. One was not mutually exclusive of the other.

271

Everywhere there were half or wholly ruined buildings, some of them uninhabited in a city where people were forced to live on the streets. There were heaps of debris and refuse. The stench of privation penetrated through the closed car windows as they drove through what should have been considered an abomination in a nation of such great wealth. This was capitalism at its worst, utterly corrupted by the putrefying misery of poverty. Yet, those who caused this misery slept peacefully in their gated communities, walled estates and guarded condominiums.

"If there is a poor man among you, one of your brothers, in any of the towns of the land which the lord your God is giving you, you shall not harden your heart, nor close your hand to your poor brother, but you shall freely open your hand to him, and generously lend him sufficient for his need in whatever he lacks." (Deuteronomy 15:7)

"Sell all your possessions and give the money to the poor, and you will have treasure in heaven." (Luke 18:22)

The abject poverty he observed made Aaron realize that the only hope in a society based on greed was a complete dismantling of the power structure. Jesus understood that those who exerted

272

a vice-like control over the country would never willingly accede to demands for fairness. It is not within the nature of those in power to willing share what they have with the less fortune, and the government and church were accomplices in the evil inequality that was allowed to flourish.

Aaron reflected back on his childhood days when he sat uninterested in Sunday school class, being propagandized and indoctrinated into judgmental arrogance. Yet, there was one verse he memorized that had always stuck with him, and the man he had put on the train in New Jersey was the living embodiment of that verse. Suddenly, Aaron looked at Mary and said, "I know why Jesus wanted to use me. I remember something I learned in Sunday School. I, Mary, am going to be the avenging sword of Jesus."

"Do not think that I came to bring peace on earth; I did not come to bring peace, but a sword." (Matthew 10:34)

273

As the Son of Thunder

CHAPTER 17
SHE FELL INTO HIS WAITING ARMS

Parking a block from his office, Aaron and Mary slowly walked down the opposite side of the street. Surveying the area for any signs of government agents, as the drizzling rain subsided, the two stood across the street from Aaron's office. Moving back under the eaves of a building to get out of the rain, they could hear themselves breathing as there was an eerie silence all about the deserted street. Noticing Sidewalk Annie's empty cart parked below his window, Aaron whispered, "I wonder where the woman who pushes that cart is? There is something weird about it just sitting there. It's not like a street person to just leave an unattended cart. You stay here, I am going in and get the notebook."

Grabbing Aaron's right arm and gripping it with both hands while putting her lips next to Aaron's right ear, in a soft, frantic voice, Mary replied, "but I want to go with you, Aaron."

Sternly, Aaron said, "O.K., but wait until I make sure it is safe. I will signal you from the window. If I don't, get the hell out of here."

Reluctantly, Mary replied, "alright."

As the Son of Thunder

Aaron methodically walked across the street with a determined stride, his hand filled with the death dealer, cocked and ready to spit flames of burning fire to sear the flesh of any in league with the evil ones who challenged the right of a man to stand against tyranny. This was no longer about Aaron, Mary, Jesus or Dixon. This was about giving a voice to those with no voice, sight to those who could not see, sustenance to those who hungered, shelter to those who shivered in the cold and compassion to those who knew none.

This man Jesus, divine or not, was the tree, and he had made Dixon, Mary and Aaron his branches to bear the fruit of his words. It was time that the money changers once again be driven from the temple. The hoarders of wealth who made slaves of the masses knew no bounds to their insatiable appetite to own more and more. That is why Jesus said that he did not come to bring peace, but to bring a sword. Only with a sword would justice be served, because those with all the power and wealth would never acquiesce to a peaceful sharing of the bounty intended for all. Aaron was the sword, and he would bring it to bear on those who had defiled the temple by turning it into a den of thievery led by the modern equivalent of the money changers. The notebook - that, too, was a mighty sword – a sword of words.

275

As the Son of Thunder

"He will sharpen his sword; He bends his bow and makes it ready. He also prepares himself instruments of death; He makes his arrows into fiery shafts." (Psalms 7:11)

"You marched through the land in indignation; You trampled the nations in anger. You went forth for the salvation of your people, for salvation with your anointed. You struck the head from the house of the wicked." (Habakkuk 3:12)

Standing erect and striding with purpose, Aaron felt that he was an uncompromising enemy of all that was wrong in a world based on the avarice pursuit of material possessions. He was about to unleash a mighty fire that would consume the evil in its path and destroy the towers of Babble erected by those who worshipped at the altar of greed. His sword was drawn and ready, and he would not sheath it until the undertaker pumped him full of embalming fluid.

Aaron rammed through the revolving door and it continued to whirl from the force he exerted as he turned right toward his office. Out of the corner of his left eye, he noticed the broom closet door slightly ajar. Gripping his revolver tightly in his right hand, he took out his key and unlocked his office door with his left hand.

276

As the Son of Thunder

He knew he had little time to get the notebook. The office had been ransacked and even the trash can had been turned over. But, there it was, deep in the bottom of the trash can. He removed the notebook, picked up a pencil from his desk and wrote across the cover, "*take to the New York Times*." To be sure it was safe from whomever he suspected was in the broom closet he went to the window and tossed it into the empty shopping cart. At the same time, he motioned for Mary to stay where she was. He dropped the pencil on the floor and turned just as Carter, Shaw and Helpern leaped through the door like bull frogs.

"The sixth angel poured out his bowl on the great river Euphrates, and its was dried up to prepare the way for the kings from the east. Then I saw three evil spirits that looked like frogs. They came out of the mouth of the beast and out of the mouth of the false prophet."(Revelation 16:12-13)

"Then they gathered the kings together to the place called Armageddon." (Revelation 16:16)

Aaron did not wait for them to fire first. He dropped to his knees behind the desk, firing one round that whizzed by the three men as they dived behind a leather sofa that sit in the left corner of the room.

Shaw broke the silence. "Adams, we just want the notebook and any copies you might have made. There is no reason for this to get out of hand. You and the woman are free to go once we have what we were sent to get. You kill one of us, and there can be no negotiations."

Aaron defiantly replied, "you and I both know that you can't let Mary and I live. With the exception of Jesus himself, we are the last real links to the truth of what went on in that chamber of horrors used by the government to extract information from the guilty and the innocent. You can't afford to let the truth get out about Jesus or about this nation's use of torture. There are still a few Americans who will not tolerate using evil to fight evil."

Shaw, almost laughing, said, "hey, we both know Jesus is no longer a problem. As for you and Mary, we can arrange to get the two of you out-of-the-country. We can arrange a stipend for you, and the two of you can live comfortably the rest of your lives."

Aaron wondered why Shaw thought Jesus was no longer a problem. What was to keep him from stirring up trouble somewhere else? There was something Aaron did not know.

278

As the Son of Thunder

Aaron leaned to the side of the desk. On the wall to his left was a mirror. In the mirror, he could see the reflection of the dim hallway light and the shadow of a woman. Was it Mary or another agent? He fretted that Mary may have decided to come into the building, in spite of his admonition to stay where she was.

Again Shaw broke the silence. "So, what is it to be, Adams? We can make a call and have a SWAT team here in five minutes, or you can give us the notebook and we can end this thing amicably."

"You and I both know you aren't calling in anybody else. You have a problem. You might actually run into some law enforcement people who won't go along with your cover-ups. Not likely, but a possibility you can't afford to risk. The only way out of this, is our deaths or yours."

Aaron heard whispering and hammers cocking. They were preparing for an assault. He had one final thing to say, and then he was going to use the last six shots he had to do as much damage as possible. "I learned a long time ago that if you don't kill the beast, the beast kills you. I am tired of assholes like you spreading terror in the name of peace. Come on and get it."

279

Aaron thought of Mary and all they had shared the past few days. He had never feared dying. Yet, he did not want to leave her. He had never believed in heaven, but wished he did, because he wanted to believe they would be together again. And what would happen to her? They would kill her, too. They had no choice in a country where the truth was feared as much as any external enemy. Aaron had no options but death for him and Mary.

Nothing is more memorable than those fleeting moments when we stand against all odds and radiate in our own righteousness. They can be momentary and fleeting, but they define our lives. Aaron was about to define his life by assuring that the truth got out. He had thrown the notebook into the shopping cart, knowing that either Sidewalk Annie or Mary would see that it was delivered to one of the few places left that believed in truth. He was ready to die now, and these bastards who served the interests of evil would go with him. He defiantly stood up from behind the desk, gun in hand.

The three men were surprised at his audaciousness. In their patriotically brainwashed minds, they could only see their duty to a cause, not their duty to truth. They, too, stood.

As the Son of Thunder

Shaw uttered, "it doesn't have to end like this Adams."

Aaron, tilting his gun toward Shaw's head, because he knew that all three were wearing bullet-proof vests, said, "the hell it doesn't," as he fired off a round that went through the top of Shaw's head, splattering brain matter against the wall. As Shaw fell backward, Carter and Helpern opened up. A bullet hit Aaron in the left shoulder and another one broke a rib as it entered his right side. Still standing, Aaron squeezed off a round that went into Helpern's right eye, glancing upward and exiting the top of his head. As Helpern fell face forward onto the sofa, Carter fired rapidly as he moved from behind the sofa toward Aaron. Feeling intense pain as bullet after bullet seemed to enter his body, Aaron continued firing, but Carter kept coming forward, even as blood poured from gapping wounds in his neck and the left side of his face. Within a few feet of Aaron, his gun simply clicked with a thud on empty chambers as he fell to the floor. Wanting to put the brave, brainwashed, clueless bastard out of his misery, Aaron aimed the gun at the back of his head and fired, but all he got was a loud thud, as he was also out of bullets.

Breathing heavily, Aaron said,"welcome to O.K.

Corral, you brave, stupid, brainwashed bastards," as he sauntered groggily backwards and rested his back against the wall beside the open window.

He stood there for awhile, just breathing heavily as pain racked his body. Looking down at the wounds, the blood flowed profusely, and he thought back on his decision to toss the notebook into the shopping cart. He glanced down at the window sill and could still see the notebook lying there in the cart, waiting to be retrieved. He had fulfilled his promise to Dixon Long, and the country would know the truth about an extraordinary man who spent a few eventful days in a small New Jersey town. Then, he looked up and in the doorway there seemed to be a translucent being, as shimmering bright rays of light appeared to emanate from above and frame the body of an angel. It was an angel. Yes, it was Mary.

The world was all before him.
The place of rest and tranquility awaited.
He would go hand-in-hand with this angel.
The darkness of this existence had faded.
He could no longer feel pain from his wounds.
The wakeful nightingale sang in the distance.
She glided toward him gracefully.
Her arms reached out to embrace his warmth.

282

As the Son of Thunder

As Aaron slide down the wall into a sitting position, his arms reached out to embrace his beloved. A shot rang out and blood splattered across Mary's white blouse as a bullet exited her chest and went into Aaron's upper left shoulder. She fell into his waiting arms.

283

EPILOGUE
THE SON OF THUNDER

Her rash hand held the weapon of deceit.
Forth from the vine she spread the evil fruit.
Earth felt the wound she inflicted.
Rising from darkness she spit fire.

The angel had been slain by evil. There in the doorway was the dragon of darkness. A cloud covered the moon and the room was bathed in blackness, as the lone flickering hallway bulb fizzled out with a soft pop. Slowly striding forward, her gun now levelled at Aaron's head, was the demon of despair – Sidewalk Annie.

Holding the angel in his arms, tears cascading down his cheeks, Aaron felt her warmth fading as the breath of life dissipated slowly. She looked up at him but could not talk. Eyes rolling back into oblivion, she left him. Clinging to her, he looked up and saw evil moving toward him.

Stopping by his desk, Annie reached up and removed her grey wig and fluffed her blond hair with a flick of the head. She removed the mouthpiece bridge that gave the illusion of missing teeth. An evil smile pursed her lips as she looked down on the lovers.

284

Evil was all about like a twisted wish. Paralyzed with shock, Aaron could taste the hate for what she had done. Feeling his angel growing stiff and cold, he knew that he had no weapons to slay the evil before him. His was a helpless fate.

Aaron looked up at the evil standing before him and said, "you're too late, bitch. I put Jesus on a train to freedom, and by now he is beyond the reach of you fascist bastards."

Annie, her eyes staring like piercing daggers ready to plunge deep into soft flesh, said, "you lying bastard. I was there when they put his lifeless body into cold storage three days ago. I still want to know why you took a dead body out of there."

Dead! Dead! The words seared into Aaron's pain-wracked brain. What were Jesus' final words from the train? "I have been crucified."

With the gun still levelled at Aaron's head, Annie whispered as she leaned closer, "you can tell me now where the notebook is, and I will end your pain."

Aaron removed his right hand from Mary's wet brow and let it rest on the floor beside him. He felt

285

As the Son of Thunder

the pencil that he had dropped earlier. He wrapped his hand around it and gripped tightly.

Looking up at Annie, he saw evil incarnate. It was not the evil of those who had been brainwashed into supporting depravity and mischief in defence of a bankrupt system of religious, monetary and patriotic servitude, but the evil of a person who enjoyed evil for evil's sake. She had been stripped bare of any redeeming light and was on the naked, dark side of a sea wracked by a war of loathsome wind. She was diabolic, grotesque and depraved like those who had led the nation astray in service to the demon of self-righteousness and the forces of darkness.

Feigning a gasp for breath, Aaron motioned with a facial movement for her to come closer so that in his weakened, dying state, she could hear his final words. She stooped down on her knees and leaned forward, levelling the gun squarely in the middle of his forehead, almost touching it, expecting to hear his final plea for mercy and a surrender of the notebook. Aaron pulled his left hand from under Mary and placed it on her now death-hardened left breast.

Keeping his voice soft and low so she would have to lean in closer, Aaron whispered, "the world

As the Son of Thunder

is a dangerous place, not because of evil, but because of those who do not fight it. I am one who fights it."

Before she could make a move, Aaron's left hand quickly swept away the gun from his forehead and it went off, searing the left side of his scalp, blood squirting profusely from the wound. Simultaneously, with his right hand, he plunged the pencil into her left temple, burying it so hard into her that it broke off half way in. She collapsed lifeless to the floor with a thud.

Kicking Annie off his legs, Aaron looked down for the last time at Mary, and he remembered some lines from an old movie. "I was born when she kissed me. I died when she left me. I lived a few weeks while she loved me."

Struggling on his knees to the window sill, he peered out into the darkness and saw the shopping cart was gone. As that deep dark pit opened up to swallow him into oblivion, he looked to his left down the street and saw a homeless man pushing the cart toward the fountain in the square. He hoped that he would do as instructed and take the notebook to the *New York Times*, so the whole world could know about the time JESUS CAME TO JERSEY AS THE SON OF THUNDER.

287

COMING SOON
from
Fireside Books
J. Wayne Frye's
New Aaron Adams Adventure

The Girl Who Stirred Up The Whirlwind

As the Son of Thunder